TAKE A BREATH AND START AGAIN

LYNNE REES

For the encouragement you gave me

To Graham, Thomas, Bethan
Mum and Dad
With Love

Vendée
Marais Poitevin
La Sèvre Niortaise
Pertuis Breton
Anse de L'Aiguillon
Charron
Les Portes-en-Ré
Esnandes
Fier d'Ars
St-Martin-de-Ré
Marsilly
Ars-en-Ré
Loix
Port du Plomb
La Couarde
La Flotte
L'Houmeau
Île de Ré
La Rochelle
Pertuis d'Antioche
Châtelaillon-Plage
Phare de Chassiron
St-Denis-d'Oléron
Réserve Naturelle du Marais d'Yves
La Brée
Île d'Aix
Fort Enet
Le Douhet
Fort Boyard
Fouras
St-Georges d'Oléron
La Charente
Boyardville
Île Madame
Fort Lupin
Rochefort-sur-Mer
St-Pierre d'Oléron
Port-des-Barques
La Cotinière
Le Château d'Oléron
Réserve Naturelle de Moëze
Île d'Oléron
Fort Louvois
Brouage
Port des Salines
Bourcefranc-le-Chapus
St-Trojan-les-Bains
Marennes
Cité de l'Huître
Pertuis de Maumusson
Moulin des Loges
Ronce-les-Bains
St-Just-Luzac
La Tremblade
La Seudre
Arvert
Chaillevette
Etaules
L'Eguille
Phare de La Coubre
Mornac-sur-Seudre
Bonne Anse
La Palmyre
Saujon
Phare de Terre-Nègre
Vaux-sur-Mer
St-Palais-sur-Mer
Royan
Phare de Cordouan
Parc de l'Estuaire
Meschers
Le Verdon-sur-Mer
Port Maran
Talmont
Les Monards
Baie de Chant-Dorat

1

Marion wore a black trouser suit and matching short woollen coat, buttoned up to keep out the damp, cold November air. Her auburn hair draped loose over her shoulders for added warmth around her neck. She sat at the old farmhouse table in the kitchen, impatiently waiting for the car that would take them to the crematorium; dreading what lay ahead. Today would not be easy for a number of reasons; the very least of them was saying goodbye to the man she married eighteen years ago. She had already done that once. She could not help feel anything except bitterness towards him. If she was right, and his death was no 'accident', all the heartache he had put them through had been for nothing.

'Why would he want to kill himself?' Her sister Carol asked. 'I thought he had everything he wanted.'

'I don't know for certain he did kill himself. It's just a hunch, something he said that night. To think, all this time I presumed he was happy. If I'd been more sympathetic we probably wouldn't have a funeral to go to.'

'The truth of the matter was that Richard had made his bed. You are no longer his wife. It wasn't your place to feel pity for him.' Carol stated as she stared out of the kitchen window towards the end of the pebble drive. The sky had turned a dark grey; she pulled at her silk scarf, tucking it tighter into her coat collar.

'I didn't feel any pity. If anything, I was even angrier with him. I don't know if I belong at this funeral or not. Do ex-wives normally go the funeral of ex-husbands?'

'I thought you said you had to go because Richard's father will be there. Speak of the devil, our carriage has arrived.'

It had been five years since Marion had seen Brian, Richard's father, and had only spoken to him briefly yesterday, when he arrived from New Zealand where he lived. They had been close, once upon a time, before he left England after the death of Richard's mother. Richard had been their only child and Marion knew what it was like to lose a child.

Carol watched the black car turn into the drive; she gave the sky one last glance. 'I hope it's not going to rain. Funerals are depressing enough without getting wet in the process.'

Brian beeped the car horn, there had been no need; the two women were already leaving the house. Marion climbed in beside him; Carol sat in the back. She had not seen Richard's father since the day of his wife's funeral. It was true what they say, how the only time you see some people are at weddings or funerals. He looked all of his seventy-one years. His hair and beard were grey, his tanned skin, heavily lined. Marion reached over and squeezed his hand. 'Welcome back. I just wish it was under better circumstances.'

He gave her a weak smile. 'Me too.'

He said very little as he drove the short distance to the crematorium. Marion left him to his thoughts whilst she wondered what he was going to make of the situation he would have to face after today. She would make sure to spend some time with him before he returned to New Zealand.

Carol leant forward to speak to her. 'What about that sleeze bag, Richard's boss. Will he be there?'

'He's meeting us at the crematorium.'

'Ugh. Should be him we're burying today.'

Brian gave Marion a quizzical look. That was something else she would probably have to explain to him.

Jodie, Marion's closest friend, had told her she would meet them there also, although Marion had told her there was no need.

'I want to. I feel I have to take some responsibility in all of this,' Jodie said.

'Why? None of it was your fault.'

'Not directly. But I sowed a seed in your mind and I can't help thinking it played a part in everything.'

Richard's father drove the car slowly through the entrance gates and down the long, sweeping drive to the parking area. A carpet of yellow and brown leaves covered the ground on either side of the drive, whilst the trees, stripped of their foliage, stood bare over them. As they stepped out of the car, a fierce gust of autumnal wind blew. Marion pulled her coat collar tighter around her neck. She nervously eyed the group of mourners waiting under cover whilst the undertakers slid the pale oak coffin out of the hearse.

There was an Aunt and Uncle of Richard's. She vaguely remembered them from his mother's side, and his work colleagues, including Paul, his boss. The remainder, she presumed, were people from Richard's new life. A life she now knew was not as happy as he had hoped it to be. The person she was expecting to see was not amongst them. Marion's eyes passed fleetingly over the grounds. She still could not see her.

She said 'Hello,' to the aunt and uncle. In a box in front of them, lay the man she had loved, and perhaps deep down, she still did. He had hurt her deeply. Right now, her feelings were more of resentment than sorrow. So much regret. Richard's father on the other hand had no time for grievances at his age. She could not help noticing the film of tears in his eyes. He would forgive Richard, even if she could not.

Marion saw her before any of them, the pale, blonde figure, in a knee length black coat and boots, looking as chic at Richard's death as she did when he was alive. She dabbed her eyes with a tissue; her vulnerability was on show for everyone to see. When she saw Marion, a shocked expression crept across her face; it almost made Marion want to smile.

Carol caught sight of her and moved protectively to stand by her sister's side, touching her arm. 'You okay?' she asked.

Marion breathed in deeply. 'I just want to get this over with.'

The woman stormed past them into the chapel, ahead of the coffin.

Marion slipped her arm into that of Brian's and waited for the coffin to pass. Swallowing hard, she remembered when she and Richard were last at the crematorium together. How she had felt like she had a hole where her stomach should be. Instead of being swollen with life, it was empty. She had wanted to give up as well, but life had moved on and somehow it had taken her with it. How could she ever have imagined what would follow, how it would all end?

They followed slowly behind with the rest of the mourners, not recognising the music that accompanied them down the aisle. If the circumstances had been different, she would have chosen Hot Chocolate, *It started with a kiss*. It had been playing when she and Richard had met, and was their first dance at their wedding. Now, as far as Marion was concerned, Richard had spoilt everything that it ever stood for between them, and he could not care less, lying there oblivious to it all.

As the coffin came to rest at the front of the chapel, the mourners filled the empty wooden pews. Jodie was late as usual, Marion smiled, Jodie would not be on time for her own funeral. She sat towards the back with Carol whilst Richard's father reluctantly walked past them to sit in the seats reserved for the family. Marion saw the blonde head of Clare in front of him. By the look she had given Marion outside, it was obvious she was not expecting her to be here today. For once, Marion felt as if she had the advantage.

At the side of the coffin, Richard's brown eyes stared out at them all from an enlarged photograph. They were the eyes that made her think of Richard Gere. Those same eyes had once shone with love for her, at times glared in hate at her, and finally lied to her. She stared back, waiting for some glimmer of emotion to emerge and reveal itself, a stinging sensation of tears in her eyes or an ache in her throat. Even though she had cried a thousand times over the last year because of Richard, the closest she came to shedding a tear today, was having to watch his father struggle to read out the eulogy, pausing every now and again to wipe away his own tears. They sang 'The Lord's My Shepherd'. Richard would have hated it, thought Marion; there was not a religious bone in his body.

When the service was over and they all filed out of the chapel, Marion sneaked one last look at Clare. Whatever it was about her she had been jealous of in the past, it no longer mattered. People's lives were not always how they seemed.

Carol followed her gaze. 'Come on, it's over.'

'She's out of your life for good now.' Jodie added.

Clare turned around as if she had heard their comments.

The three women watched as she approached them. Marion's heart began beating faster; Jodie held her chin high in a look of defiance. When Clare got closer, Carol linked her arm through Marion's as a show of solidarity.

'He was with you, wasn't he? The night he … Why did he come to see *you*? I want to know.'

Marion was stunned for a moment. How did Clare know about Richard's visit to her house? She saw Clare fight to control the tears and would have taken great delight in seeing her face crumble even more if she told her the reason he came. Instead, she took some satisfaction from knowing that Clare was having to swallow her pride right now; remembering their initial meeting when it had been her turn. Reluctantly, she decided this was not the time for recriminations. Richard had created enough damage when he was alive. She knew from experience it was best if some things remained buried.

'It wasn't important,' she told Clare. 'There is nothing for you to worry about.' Then she allowed her sister to guide her away as another gust of cold wind wrapped itself around them.

'Why didn't you tell her?' Carol asked as they made their way back to the car.

'What purpose would it serve today or any day?' Marion said.

'Because she deserves to have to live with the truth.'

'Do you really think adding insult to injury is a good thing? We both know what it's like to live with regret.'

'Exactly my point! Why should she of all people get away with it? You're going soft.'

Brian was waiting in the car for them. 'Is everything alright? Only I saw you with …'

'Everything's fine,' Marion told him.

'I'm going to have to speak to her sometime soon,' he said.

She squeezed his hand. 'I know you are.'

He drove the car slowly up the drive towards the road. The wind shook the branches of the trees; the remaining leaves that had clung on to them fell to the ground.

Marion took one last look behind her. '*Goodbye Richard*'. The first tears of the day stung her eyes.

As he stopped to wait for traffic, Brian gave her a sympathetic smile. 'What will you do now?' he asked.

Marion thought for a moment. Whichever way she looked at her life, she had a new beginning ahead of her, a chance to get it right this time.

'Ensure I have no more regrets,' she replied.

Making the right choice was what mattered now, even if it turned out not to be the one she wanted. Nobody else new of the decision she still had to make or the person who was waiting for her answer.

2

Eight months earlier.

Spring arrived in Huddersfield. An otherwise grey canvas was brought to life by cheery yellow daffodils alongside lilac and orange crocuses.

The town, once the heart of the textile mills and the industrial revolution, nestled between the Pennine Hills and the Peak District. A statue of Harold Wilson stood in the square in front of the railway station.

Marion and Richard lived ten minutes out of the centre, twenty minutes when the traffic lights were all on red. The house, an old, stone, detached cottage, had a gravel driveway to the front, and at the back, a wooden shed occupied the corner of a flagstone terrace.

Marion was in the bedroom, rummaging amongst the contents of her underwear drawer for something to wear. She had been meaning to tidy it up for ages. There must be at least four bras she never wore anymore and umpteen odd socks. As she pushed the contents around, her fingers touched the grainy black and white scan of a baby at twenty weeks old, alive, growing inside her. It was hidden away in the drawer from Richard, who she knew, would only insist she got rid of it.

She brought the image to her lips, as she always did in a sort of ritual; the tears welled up. She wanted to stop. She had tried, knowing it wasn't helping her get over what happened. She was afraid if she did stop, she would forget all about Anna. Thank God, they had already chosen a name; it was from Marion's favourite childhood book, *Anne of Green Gables*. At least it meant she could hold onto something tangible.

There was a lavender scented bag at the back of the drawer, she placed the image underneath and covered it up with the rest of her underwear.

A car horn beeped in the drive.

Hastily, she pulled on a pair of leggings and a sweatshirt, pulling her hair back into a ponytail, before looking out of the bedroom window to see Richard taking what appeared to be a cat basket from the back seat of the car. Intrigued, she hurried downstairs and out onto the drive.

Richard had opened the front of the basket and was reaching inside. He pulled out a bundle of fur.

'Oh, it's adorable!' Marion reached out her hands and gently lifted the tiny black and white kitten from Richard. It crawled up her shoulder, burying its head under her chin.

'I thought it might cheer you up. She's something you can mother in the mean time.'

Marion registered 'in the meantime' then let it go.

'The vet has given her all the vaccinations and a micro chip, in case we lose her.'

'Does she also have a name?'

'I'll leave that up to you.'

'What do we feed her on? How old is she?' Marion stroked the kitten along its back, burying her cheek into its head.

'Four months old,' Richard shouted over his shoulder as he opened the back door of the car, and fetched out a cardboard box with a fur lined cat bed balancing on the top. 'Everything you need is in here.'

Marion followed him into the house. The kitten, sensing she was on the move, clung even tighter to her neck.

Richard placed the bed on the terracotta- tiled floor, next to the radiator. Marion prized the kitten away from her and put it in the middle of the bed. Dazed, it stood for a moment then sat down watching, as Richard took a bag of dried food from the box followed by two small stainless steel bowls. Filling one with water and the other with food, he left them by the side of the bed.

The kitten did not move. Marion tickled it behind the ears and it lifted its face so she could tickle its chin. 'She seems to like that. I'm going to call her Mimi.'

'Well, Mimi,' Richard said to the cat, 'be prepared to be spoilt.' He put his arms around Marion's waist and kissed her briefly on the lips. 'Did I do the right thing?'

Marion looked at Mimi who, having ventured out of her bed was lapping at the water bowl. 'Do you know, I think for once you might have.' She laughed. Whilst Richard set up Mimi's litter tray, she made coffee. Then she sat down and lifted Mimi onto her lap. Whenever Marion stroked her, Mimi purred loudly.

3

It had been raining heavy since the early hours. At peak rush hour, around 8 a.m., a lorry skidded and jack-knifed across all three lanes of the M62 motorway at Ainley Top, approximately ten minutes from Huddersfield Royal Infirmary where the Accident and Emergency department was poised ready to receive the injured.

Marion had worked in the department, as a nurse for nearly twenty years. Although demanding, tiring and at times emotional, she loved her job. When she left school at eighteen, she had no idea what she wanted to do so had applied for a job with the Halifax Building Society, because everyone else she knew was doing the same. The position bored her within a year. It was her mother, who persuaded her to give nursing a go and she had never looked back.

Her first patient from the accident was a seven-year-old boy with concussion. The triage doctor had assessed him and Marion was keeping him under observation.

Sister Harding beckoned her over.

'The poor mite,' she said. 'I've just been informed his mother died in surgery. His father is on his way in.'

'Why is it always the children that get to us the most,' Marion said. 'In one respect I guess I should be thankful we haven't got any. You never know what's around the corner.'

Sister Harding smiled in sympathy. 'It's not too late. Don't let what happened put you off.'

Marion half smiled as if she agreed.

What did the Sister know about it?

Through the rain soaked window, she watched the small, blonde figure of Jodie running towards the hospital entrance. She had pulled her umbrella down close to her head but barely succeeding in keeping any part of her dry.

She must be on 'afters' thought Marion as she watched her disappear through the doors where she would take the lift to the Paediatric ward.

What would she have done without her best friend these past months?

*

In an effort to stay looking younger, Richard had taken to visiting the gym twice a week in his lunch hour. Five miles and one of them up hill, he was getting better on the running machine each time. He had toned shoulder and arm muscles; though a long way from being like Arnold Schwarzenegger, and unlike his boss, he had avoided the dreaded beer belly. The only thing he wished for now was that his brown, curly hair would stop receding.

He sat down to get his breath.

Paul put down the dumb bells. Having wiped the sweat from his neck and forehead with his towel, he wondered over to join him.

'You still okay for tomorrow night?' he asked. 'Marion was alright with the idea wasn't she?'

'Yes she's looking forward to it.' Richard lied. He had not had the courage to tell Marion anything about Paul's suggestion that they go out one evening to discuss his possible move to becoming Operational Director of the haulage company.

'How is she coping after …'

'Fine.' He lied again.

He felt uneasy talking about something so personal with Paul, even though he had known him for the past twenty years. He started as a driver for Roberts Ltd, a company founded by Paul's grandfather when he was twenty-five. At thirty-five, he was promoted to Warehouse Manager, and now, at nearly forty-five, he hoped his devotion to the company was about to be recognised.

Wanting desperately to avoid any further conversation, Richard slung his towel over his shoulder and made a move towards the changing rooms.

'See you at seven, at the Rose and Crown.' Paul shouted after him.

Richard showered and dressed. If everything went to plan, soon he would be putting on a suit instead of a pair of jeans and a t-shirt, and he could look forward to swapping his Peugeot for the black BMW Series 3 he had always wanted. He and Marion had not had an easy time lately. He was pleased he had bought the kitten for her, perhaps now she would show some enthusiasm for life again. He was confident this new position in the company was a move in the right direction; he could sense it was going to be the start of better times to come.

Marion was stretched out on the cherry red sofa in the living room, the one she had persuaded Richard to buy in the sale at Next; the one he hated, when he arrived home from work. A *Woman and Home* magazine lay open across her stomach; a sleeping kitten curled under her chin.

Marion opened her eyes as Richard entered the room.

He dropped a magazine onto the oak coffee table and bent to kiss her forehead, before going to hang his coat up in the hall.

Richard never bought Magazines; he thought they were a waste of money and grumbled every time Marion bought one. Curious, she raised her head to see what he had dropped onto the table.

'Why have you bought a magazine about cars?'

'Because I've got something to tell you.'

He lifted her feet, sat down and placed them on his knees. 'How would you like it if I became Operational Director of the haulage company?' He beamed.

Marion said nothing at first.

'Did you hear what I just said?'

'Has Paul put you up to this?'

'I thought you'd be pleased. He's invited us out with him, and what's his wife's name?'

'Sandra.'

'To discuss it.'

He watched as her face fell further than it had when he made the announcement. 'I know how you're still feeling, but this is important to me. Please say you'll go.'

Marion sighed. 'Sandra talks about nothing except her children. I know I shouldn't feel jealous …'

She stroked Mimi, who had snuggled tighter into her shoulder. 'You go.'

'I didn't get you a cat so you could use it as an excuse not to go out. She was fine today whilst we were at work. We'll leave the lamp on. Nothing is going to happen to her.'

Why couldn't he see she wasn't ready to do the whole socialising thing, and especially not with Paul and Sandra. She barely knew Sandra. They had met only once before at one of Richard's Christmas parties and she had talked incessantly about her two children then.

'What if they want to talk about…'

'They won't. We're going there to discuss me; my future, our future.'

20

He massaged her feet. 'I do love you. There's no need to spend the evening worrying about the cat.'

Marion was not concerned about Mimi. If anyone else told her that they were sorry for her loss, she would scream. She was envious of Richard. Life had returned to normal for him.

When would that ever be the case for her?

As if reading her thoughts, Richard said softly, 'We have to move on.'

'I can't move on like you. It's not that easy.'

Richard gave her a look. She knew it meant 'stop all this nonsense', and said, 'So, are we having a night out?

The phone rang in the hall.

Richard sighed, annoyed at being interrupted at such a crucial moment.

'It's Carol, he said. No doubt, she wants a favour from you, as always.'

Marion exchanged Mimi for the phone.

Richard immediately put the cat on the floor; he was not into cuddling animals. He preferred obedient dogs that lay at your feet and did not move unless commanded to do so.

Carol seemed subdued. She asked if Marion minded if she sent Alice round for tea at the weekend.

'Of course I don't mind, but a teenager wanting to spend Saturday night with her aunt …surely she has a boyfriend she'd rather be with?'

Marion's niece was seventeen, a bright, confident girl in the middle of her 'A' level studies. Marion was especially fond of her and was aware this did not always please her sister. There had to be a good reason she was asking if Alice could visit.

'I don't know anything about that, but while she's there, try and find out what's wrong at school will you? Her grades are nowhere near as good as they used to be. She's miserable all the time. She won't open up to us.' There was a slight pause. 'No doubt she'll talk to you. You two have always been close.'

Marion caught the sarcasm in Carol's voice. 'I'll expect her around five,' she told her and ended the call.

'Alice is coming for tea.'

'Is that such a good idea?' Richard said. 'You know how your sister feels about you and Alice.'

'For your information, Carol asked if she could come.'

4

Standing in front of the full-length mirror, Marion passed her hands over her stomach. It was hard to believe she had ever been pregnant. Her body showed no outward signs and she slipped easily in to her old pair of jeans before pulling on a black jumper that was at least three years old. Uncaringly, she pulled a brush through her hair, scraped it back into the usual ponytail, and secured it with the same black velvet band she used for work. Her make-up remained untouched. Despite this minimum amount of effort, and to the annoyance of Richard, she deliberately took her time to get ready for their night out.

'Hurry up will you, we'll be late.'

Good! She wanted to shout back. It was childish but the later they were, the less time they would have to spend at the pub. She had a niggling feeling the evening was going to be a disaster.

In the kitchen, Richard had put on his coat and was loitering impatiently. She felt the icy blast from the already opened door.

His eyes passed fleetingly over what she was wearing. He did not have to say anything. She just could not find the will to make an effort these days.

The Rose and Crown pub, built from Yorkshire stone, stood exposed, on the top of Cop Hill high above Huddersfield. It looked down on the village of Slaithwaite and the rest of the Colne Valley. Dry stone walls divided the green fields that could be seen for miles around it.

Richard drove cautiously up the steep, winding road from the valley bottom. They passed lambs frolicking in the lush grass, stopping only to suckle from their mother.

Marion watched them, their tiny tails bobbing from side to side, as they buried their heads to search out the milk.

She would still have been breast-feeding Anna now.

As she stepped out of the car in the car park, the fresh breeze chilled her. She pulled her jacket tight and hurried inside the pub.

There was a fire roaring in the wood burner. She made a beeline for it and stood, warming herself. The smell of gourmet cooking floated in the air. They had eaten here often. She surveyed the choice of meals on the blackboard pinned to the wall. There were still the regular favourites: Fish and Chips, Steak and Ale pie, and Scampi, a favourite of her mothers.

Paul and Sandra sat at a table close to the window, with their drinks. The view was of the outside terrace with tables and wooden benches. Spring bulbs poked out of the top of old wooden beer barrels, used as plant pots.

Richard had hardly spoken to her on the way here, and judging from the amount Paul had already drunk from his pint, Marion guessed that meant they were late. Reluctantly she left the warmth of the fire to sit with them.

Paul was a big man, with sandy coloured hair, a broad chest and shoulders matched by the beginnings of a beer belly. Sandra was dark and petite. She looked even smaller sitting next to her husband. She smiled as Marion sat down opposite her.

Marion forced a friendly smile back

Richard returned from the bar having presumed what Marion wanted to drink. A glass of red wine appeared in front of her. She took a sip; it was dry and acidic. She felt the burning sensation as it passed down to her stomach. It was house wine, the cheapest of the cheap. She knew they served her favourite *Shiraz*, as did Richard. He also knew how uncomfortable this was for her, yet so far, he had made no effort to ease the situation. She wanted the ground to open up and swallow her.

For a few seconds, there was an awkward silence between the four of them until Sandra turned to Marion and placed a hand on her arm. 'I'm sorry about the baby.'

Marion cursed inwardly. 'Thank you,' she replied, praying that was all she would have to endure on the subject.

'Will you try again?'

Marion's heart missed a beat as she shrank back and tensed.

Sandra had no right to ask something so intimate.

She looked pleadingly at Richard. He was staring at her with an impatient almost hostile look.

'I don't see why not,' he said suddenly.

Marion stared back at him in shock, not caring if it was only bravado in front of his boss. He had no right to say such a thing. They had not even talked about it together, and it was the first time Richard had indicated he wanted another child.

The urge to get up and run was overwhelming; she turned to look out of the window, tears and anger welled up inside her. A row of daffodils dancing freely in the breeze in one of the barrels held her attention for a moment, then she took a sip of the acidic wine to try to calm down.

Why had she let Richard talk her into coming?

She waited for him to say something, at least make a show of his concern for how she was feeling. Instead, he ignored her, preferring to talk work with Paul.

Sandra, oblivious to the upset she had just instigated, insensitively tried to make conversation about her children.

Marion wanted to shout at Paul, 'For God's sake! Give Richard the job so we can all go home.'

Finally, she had her wish and they left the pub.

Richard climbed inside the car and slammed the door shut. Marion jumped at the noise.

'Why were you so rude to Sandra?' He demanded.

'When was I rude?'

'She asked about us having another baby, you ignored her.'

'I told you I didn't want to talk about it.'

'And I didn't want this evening ruined. Why can't you stop dwelling on Anna for once.'

She stared at him. Tears stung her eyes. She could not believe he was talking to her like this; how different he suddenly was. 'You're the one in the wrong. We haven't even talked about having another child. Why did you tell them we would?'

'Well why can't we? It doesn't mean it will happen a second time. The doctors said as much.'

'But they couldn't guarantee it,' she said unyieldingly. 'Are you willing to take that risk?'

'Aren't you?'

At that moment, an image sprang into Marion's mind of a tiny, white coffin and two pink roses on the top. She brushed the tears away with her fingers.

'I want her back so much it aches. It doesn't stop.'

'And you think I don't feel anything, is that it?'

'I don't think it's the same for you. It's all about work now.'

Richard pulled at his seat belt. 'So what are you trying to say?'

She found it difficult to look at him and stared ahead out of the car window into the darkness that surrounded them. It would be the shortest day soon, the evenings would start to draw out. She had suffered many sleepless nights battling with the decision whether to try again. Finally, she had reached a conclusion.

'I'm going to be forty soon, it's too much of a risk.'

'No more than before and you were willing to carry on then.'

'We shouldn't have put off having a family, we left it too late. Maybe this is our punishment.'

'Don't be stupid! It was just bad luck.'

'You call losing a child bad luck?'

'What else would you call it? There was no medical reason. The doctor said it was just one of those things.'

She could not believe how flippant he was being. 'I couldn't bear it if the same thing happened.'

'So that's it. As per usual, there's no discussion, *You've* decided.'

Why did he have this way of always making her feel guilty? As if somehow, it was all her fault.

'I'm sorry. It's how I feel.'

They drove back home in silence. When they walked in to the kitchen, Mimi opened her eyes without raising her head from the basket. Marion liked the French name; it seemed perfect for something so small.

Maybe this tiny black and white bundle of fur would help her get over her grief.

She went over to stroke her. There was evidence she had used the cat litter tray whilst they had been out, a sign she was settling herself into her new home.

'I wish we hadn't gone tonight,' Marion said.

'I told you we were there for me.' Richard sighed angrily. 'Is this how it's going to be from now on, all about you? Maybe you should think about seeing one of your hospital shrinks.'

5

The following morning, after having barely spoken to each other since Richard's cutting comment about her need to seek psychiatric help, which she had to admit he might be right, Marion came downstairs to find him sat at the kitchen table, shovelling down cereal as fast as he could. It was a surprise to find him there, normally he was long gone by now.

'You're late,' she said.

'Yes, thank you. I'm well aware,' he said in between mouthfuls. 'Why didn't you set the alarm? Some of us don't have the luxury of starting work half way through the day.'

'I did tell you I was on the late shift, besides you'll have the luxury of knowing I'm still working when you're tucked up in bed.'

He got up without answering her, left his bowl where it was and hastily put on his jacket, uttered an unfeeling 'Bye,' gave her a perfunctory kiss on the cheek and disappeared out of the door.

'Bye,' she muttered under her breath.

His reaction to her working the late shift came as no surprise since her absence meant he would be on his own in the evening, and would have to cook for himself or heat up a microwave meal for one. She knew he would not even do that. She had given him the perfect excuse to go to the local pub.

A black leg with a white paw on the end of it, and a small, black head appeared under the raised cat flap in the kitchen door. Mimi stopped and surveyed the room before entering. Marion knew she was looking to see if Richard was around. He seemed to have fallen out with both of them. The cat curled herself around Marion's leg and purred softly. She bent down and picked the kitten up. 'I suppose you want your breakfast as well?'

She placed a handful of dried food in Mimi's bowl and poured a small amount of milk into the saucer next to it. 'It's a good job I've got you. I'm beginning to feel you're the only one that wants me around.'

*

Paul had told Richard, he would start his new job as Operational Director within the month. As one of the big boys, he would make the decisions now, and have his own secretary to run round after him.

He planned to buy two suits from Austin Reed in Leeds city centre, one navy and one charcoal grey and place an order at the BMW garage. Soon, he could look forward to driving his brand new car.

Perhaps, he had been a little harsh on Marion last night. He should have apologised to her about what he had said in the pub. It was all because he did not want to appear inadequate in Paul's eyes. God knows why. Clearly, the fault did not lie with him; Marion would not have got pregnant if he was to blame. There was also another reason, he hated to admit it, but he genuinely did want to try again for another child. Like Marion, he had been happy to go on holiday year after year, but now he had had a taste of nearly becoming a father, he found he could not let it go. He could not see why Marion continued dwelling on the past; it seemed pointless. Other things had begun to annoy him too, like when was the last time he had seen her in a dress? She wore leggings all the time now with a shapeless jumper. He remembered buying her some nice underwear one Christmas. He had never seen it again since she had unwrapped it.

What was that saying? 'Shit happens'. Well, it happened five months ago and in his opinion life had to carry on, which was exactly why, after finishing work and not in the mood to go home to an empty house, he decided to go for a drink.

It was a mere two minute walk from his office to the *Dog and Duck* close to the railway arches in Leeds. Far enough, on a cold, dark evening when the air was damp with drizzle.

The pub, an old fashioned boozer with treacle coloured wall paper, dark furnishings, and ancient nicotine stains on the ceilings, was one of the few that had not been turned into a trendy wine bar and restaurant.

As he opened the door, the warmth met him along with competing whiffs of perfume and aftershave. Men had discarded their ties and jackets over the backs of chairs or folded them up on seats. The whole place was alive with conversation and laughter.

Richard recognised some of the people from the firm of solicitors that occupied the first floor of a red brick building about 200 yards away from his office. At lunchtime, they would occasionally queue together for the takeaway sandwich and burger van that toured the industrial estate.

A young, attractive, blonde woman smiled at him. He smiled back, ordered a pint of Tetley's beer then propped himself against the bar knowing the alternative to being here was a microwave meal for one in front of the TV.

Someone had left *The Sun* newspaper folded in half on the bar. He was a *Daily Express* man but he liked the sports pages in *The Sun*. He was reading about the latest football revelation when the blonde woman appeared at the bar next to him. She wore a grey pencil skirt with a tight white blouse and there was no way he could ignore her cleavage. She hoisted herself onto a vacant bar stool next to him and as her skirt rode up, he noticed the bit of nicely shaped thigh that was now on show.

Richard held out his glass for the barman to refill it.

'Drinking on your own?' she asked. 'I could keep you company.'

'If you don't mind me saying, you don't look like the sort of girl that frequents this type of pub.'

'You're not wrong. Give me a nice Chardonnay in a classy wine bar any day. It's that lot.' She nodded her head towards the small group of people he had seen her with earlier.

'The beer is good and cheap so we have to come here.'

'And the wine?'

'It's shit!'

Richard laughed. He glanced over to her companions. A lanky, dark haired man, with a big nose glared back at him. Richard put him at about thirty.

'I don't think I'm very popular with your friend.'

She pulled a face. 'Just ignore him. I made the mistake of making him a coffee one day, now he thinks I'm interested in him.'

'And are you?'

She smiled at Richard. 'What do you think?'

'I think you're using me to make your escape.'

'Does it bother you?'

'What do you think?'

They both laughed.

'I'm Clare.' She held out her hand, he noticed her baby blue eyes. 'And I'll have a gin and slimline tonic, please… no ice.'

'Richard,' he said as he shook her hand then ordered her a drink.

'Haven't I seen you before?'
'You mean I'm not etched on your memory?'
He smiled. 'You work next door.'
'For old Mr Billingham, the solicitor. I'm his secretary.'

Lucky him, thought Richard. All I get is a butch woman with short, ginger hair, who probably prefers women to men.

For the next hour, he found himself enjoying her attentiveness. Her hair, cut in a bob shape, framed her pretty face. She had a habit of pushing it back behind her ears and he noticed the long, bright red, manicured nails and the absence of any rings. He wanted to ask if there was any one waiting at home for her, after all, she would have seen that he was married yet that had not stopped her from flirting with him.

He felt a touch of excitement.

They finished their drinks and Clare went to say goodbye to the group she came with then left with Richard.

He could feel the eyes of the man with the big nose, burning into his back.

Outside, the drizzle had stopped but the air was dank. Clare pulled on a pair of black leather gloves. Richard dug his hands deep into the pockets of his overcoat.

'Thank you for the drink.' She smiled.
'It was my pleasure. Goodnight.'
'Goodnight.'

She made no move to leave.

Reluctantly, Richard turned to walk away.

'If you're at a loose end,' she called after him, 'we usually come here for a drink after work.'

He stopped and turned to look back at her, holding her gaze. Then he smiled and walked on.

6

Marion knew Richard would be home from work in half an hour and he would expect her to cook dinner.

She changed into a pair of comfortable black leggings and a sweatshirt then poured herself a glass of red Shiraz. With a resigned sigh, she began preparing the vegetables. After, she poured a second glass of wine and stared absent-mindedly at them bobbing up and down in the boiling water, before realised there was a muffled ringing sound coming from her handbag.

She rummaged frantically for her phone but it was too late.

Richard had been put through to voice mail.

Knowing he would not be pleased and that she would have to ring him back, she took a gulp of wine.

'Do you ever answer your bloody phone? It's always at the bottom of that sack of yours.'

'Sorry,' she mumbled.

'I won't be home for dinner; I've got to supervise a late delivery.'

'Again?'

She looked at the vegetables that were nearly cooked and the shepherd's pie browning in the oven, she stopped herself from telling him it was a bit late to be cancelling dinner after she had slaved away and done a days work herself. Nor did she ask why his Warehouse Manager was unable to do the job instead of him. If she did, she would be questioning his actions and that would annoy him more.

She moved to switch off the gas.

'I'll get something to eat before I come home. Don't wait up.' He ended the call.

She downed the last drop of wine in her glass and without hesitating, reached for the bottle and poured herself another. It no longer mattered what time dinner was ready; she could relax now, eat when she wanted to. It was nothing new for Richard to work late these days, so she was no stranger to preparing a meal for two then eating alone. He obviously considered the food at the local pub to be better than her cooking because he always ended up there.

She went upstairs to run a bath.

With its cream, shag pile carpet and scented candles, the *en suite* bathroom was Marion's sanctuary. She added some Jo Malone bath oil to the water; it filled the room with a heady scent of citrus. She lay down in the warm water and let the bubbles cover her from head to toe in a white blanket.

Richard's brown eyes were what had first attracted her to him. They reminded her of the actor, Richard Gere. What she had liked most about him, was the way he fooled around in jest. On her first day at work as a newly qualified nurse, he had sent her a bouquet of flowers, a mixture of red roses, cream carnations and pink lilies. He had written a silly poem on the card and his telephone number; she could still memorise every word.

On New Years Eve we stopped and stared, now I wonder if I dare, hope that you would like, to come out with me one night.

The card was in her bedside drawer with all the rest of the romantic ones he had sent her, some with a personal message from him that was poignant to their relationship. On top of that, he called her everyday without fail and bought her flowers each week.

She recalled the feeling of being deeply in love. Now she felt very much alone.

Richard was always working and had become distant. She tried to think back to the last time they had made love and could not recall.

What if it was she who had distanced herself from him and was to blame for the way they had grown apart?

She rummaged at the back of one of her drawers and found the three-quarter length, black, silk negligee Richard had bought her one Christmas. She remembered wearing it that night. Being long it had twisted around her legs each time she turned over; she forever had to tug it free.

She slipped the negligee on and climbed into bed, picked up her book and waited for Richard to come home.

It was close to ten-thirty when she heard him come upstairs and go into the bathroom. Finally, he climbed into bed beside her. He had a pile of papers with him.

She turned to face him expecting the usual peck on the cheek he gave her when he returned from work. When he made no move to kiss her, she moved further down the bed, closer to him and laid her arm around his waist.

'I forgot to tell you, Carol rang last week while you were on nights,' he said.'

'What did she want?'

'I didn't ask. I'm not your secretary.'

Marion raised her head from the pillow. 'What is it with you and my sister?'

'I don't know why you're getting all defensive. She doesn't like you very much,' he said.

Marion removed her arm from around him and sat back up. 'What's that supposed to mean?'

'You know very well. You're stepping on her toes as far as your niece is concerned.'

'Rubbish! Did she tell you this?'

'She doesn't have to. It's obvious to me.'

'You don't know what you're talking about; you don't have a sister or a brother.'

'Or a mother or a father,' he added.

'You do have a father.'

'On the other side of the world, in New Zealand!'

'You were happy when he took his future life into his own hands after your mum died. You said, it was one less responsibility you would have to bear. I know there was no point in inviting him to Anna's funeral, but secretly I hoped he would come back to see us. Even stay permanently. I miss him.'

When she first met Richard's father he hugged her. She found it an odd gesture for the first time they had met. Later, she found out both his parents thought she was the best thing that had happened to Richard in a long while; that he had finally met his match with her.

Richard's mother had a placid personality and a heart of gold; she didn't think ill of anyone. When she died of cancer, Marion felt her heart would burst with sadness. In the crematorium, she had wanted to be strong for Richard, she held his hand for the duration of the service but it was she, who had sobbed. Afterwards, she had linked her arm through Richard's fathers and they had cried together.

Richard did not cry at all that day.

A month after his mother's death, he told her how he had gone into the local church to light a candle for her and sobbed quietly on his own.

She thought his father would never get over his wife's death until one day he announced he was moving. She was horrified. Her own father had died along time ago from an aneurism. It felt like she was losing him all over again.

'He wants us to go and live in New Zealand. He thinks moving is the answer to everything. A fresh start...'

'You never told me this.'

'There was no point. We're not going. The grass is the same colour over there as it is in West Yorkshire. Anyway, it was different for Dad, he needed to get away from forty-five years of memories; he didn't feel he could move on if he stayed. Our life is here and I don't feel the need to run away.'

Richard began to rifle through the papers.

'Why have you brought those to bed with you?'

'Because I can't find a letter from one of our customers. Have you been tidying up again? I'm certain I left it on the kitchen table.'

Marion sighed, 'I haven't seen a letter.'

Richard shot her an impatient look. 'You must have. I remember putting it down.'

He threw the papers on the floor. 'Are you sure you haven't moved it?'

She paused to think. Richard had a way of making her doubt herself even when she was certain she was right.

'Yes, I'm sure.'

He jumped out of bed.

'Where are you going?'

'To look for it. You'll have put it somewhere. Why can't you bloody well leave things alone?'

He stomped out of the room.

7

Carol's words played on Marion's mind. She did not like the thought that Alice was not happy at school; it was so out of character. She let out a squeal of delight when Alice stepped into the kitchen, and wrapped her arms around what there was of her niece. The mustard coloured jumper she wore hung loose as if it was a size too big. Alice had never carried any weight but she appeared to Marion to be even thinner.

Alice was tall, 5'7", with long shapely legs. Underneath the peaky mask was a pretty girl with honey-blond tresses and beautiful, brown eyes. She had not finished maturing but Marion could tell she was going to grow into something quite special.

'I thought we'd order pizza from the takeaway.' Marion picked up a leaflet from the kitchen worktop. 'Here, have a look. What do you fancy?'

Alice dropped into a chair at the kitchen table, and studied the leaflet briefly before handing it back to her aunt.

Marion noticed her fingernails were virtually non-existent. The image of an excited teenager on her sixteenth birthday sprang into her mind. Long, beautifully manicured nails, all multicoloured were dangled in front of her.

'Aren't they gorgeous?' Alice had enthused. 'Mum paid for me to have a manicure for my birthday.'

'So, how is school these days? Are you still playing sport? What is it… netball and hockey?

'Not any more I gave it up.'

'Oh! Why's that? I thought you enjoyed it.'

'I did…but not now. Some of the girls just fool around; it's not as much fun as it used to be.'

'Fooling around in a nice way or a bad way?' Marion asked.

'They're not very nice girls.' Alice mumbled.

'What about your lessons?'

'They're ok.'

'Still heading for those good grades I hope. I'm always telling people how clever you are. You're doing all right aren't you?'

Alice fidgeted in the chair. 'Yeh, I suppose. I've been ill a few times. I've had to miss some lessons.

'Your mum never said. What's been wrong with you?'

'Oh, Y' know, headaches, stomach aches. Mum thinks it's just my hormones.'

'Have you seen a doctor, just to be sure?'

'No, Mum says there's no need; it's just my age.'

Mum thinks, mum says; was Carol really that blind! The chewed nails, the weight loss, the sallow complexion. Why had she not noticed any of these …and what about sport? Alice had been chosen to play in all the school teams as far back as Marion could remember. Now, because of some girls, she had suddenly stopped.

'Maybe it is just your hormones,' Marion smiled reassuringly.

'Can I go and put the telly on?' Alice was already walking into the living room with Mimi in tow.

It was obvious to Marion that was the end of the conversation but she had seen and heard enough. Pursuing the subject would most likely spoil the evening and her time with Alice was precious.

She went to ring for the pizza. Carol had asked her to find out what was wrong. Marion knew she would not like the answer she was going to give her.

*

Marion tried to relax. The brown soft leather armchair was comfortable, and she was neither too hot nor too cold. Cream roller blinds that stopped half way down their length softened the light from two windows. The atmosphere was almost cosy; she did not feel like she was in the spotlight.

'How are you today Marion?'

This was her second session with Doctor Lamont. He did not pronounce the 't' at the end of his name. When she had enquired why not, he told her that was how it was pronounced in French, and when she asked why he was in England, he told her, 'England was short of doctors so I came to help and stayed.' His smile was as broad as he was tall, and the frames of his glasses matched his dark hair. He was attentive, did not annoy her by writing secret notes whilst she spoke, he simply listened, occasionally swapping over his long crossed legs. Maybe he did not need to write anything down. Maybe there was a model answer to her problem; she would not be the first to experience such a trauma. He would ask her a set of questions then come up with a set of answers, she would thank him and go away cured of her grief, able to put it all behind her just as Richard had.

'I'm fine.' She lied. She was far from it. She had lost a child, did not want to have another and risk it happening again. She had expected her husband to agree with her decision. He had not agreed and further more had literally screamed at her to go and see a psychiatrist.

'What does your husband do for work?'

'He recently became a director at a haulage company.'

'And how do you feel about that?'

'Happy. Of course.'

Doctor Lamont looked pensive for a moment and scratched his cheek.

'Does the fact that despite losing a child he can still carry on achieving something for himself upset you?'

'Do you mean am I jealous because he continues to succeed in what he does whilst I failed to produce a child? Yes. Why does he have to make me feel like he's rubbing my nose in it?'

If only she and Richard had not carried on arguing about that damn letter. When he finally found it, there was no apology; instead, he had snored away at the side of her whilst she had spent another sleepless night wondering just how much more she could take.

When she left Dr Lamont, she still had no idea where all this would lead, if anywhere. She drove straight to the hospital and went to the canteen, where she spotted Jodie sat at one of the tables. She queued for her coffee and carried it over. With a tired sigh, she flopped into a hard wooden chair opposite her.

Jodie threw her a surprised look. 'Have I missed something?' she asked.

'What do you mean?'

'We've known each other for twenty two years, since when has chocolate not been part of your staple daily diet?'

Marion managed a weak smile. 'I'm not hungry this morning, that's all.'

'What's wrong?' Jodie asked.

'Richard's got me seeing a psychiatrist.' Marion saw the blueberry muffin on Jodie's plate. 'I thought you wanted to lose weight?'

'Don't change the subject. Why are you seeing a shrink?'

Marion was not in the mood to go into details of why she had decided to see Dr Lamont. She looked down to her lap and twisted the gold band on her finger. She had left her engagement ring in the mahogany jewellery box because she had somehow lost the centre stone from the diamond cluster. She considered it poignant that the ring was falling apart along with her marriage. She needed to know if she was overreacting to everything.

'Can I ask you something? What would you do if Kevin accused you of moving something you hadn't even seen? Then didn't believe you when you said you hadn't.'

Jodie laughed. 'I'd suggest that he'd carried out a man look, and send him to search for it again.'

Marion smirked. Jodie's husband was easy going, perhaps too much to be a police officer, and in complete contrast to his feisty wife. She could imagine him doing as he was told. If only it was that simple with Richard.

'Why?' Jodie quizzed her. 'What are you supposed to have moved?'

'We ended up arguing last night over a stupid letter.'

'A letter! Is that all?'

'I know. Pathetic isn't it.'

'Well, was it an important letter, a life and death kind of thing?'

'No nothing like that. It was only from a customer. 'Why can't I just bloody well leave things alone?' She said, mimicking Richard. 'That was his parting shot before he stormed off. What's even more annoying, I knew he would find it on the desk in the study; it's like a table at a jumble sale, there are papers everywhere.'

She took a sip of her coffee. 'It's like he's trying to make me pay the price everyday for … as if I don't feel guilty enough. You'd expect such a misfortune as losing a baby to have brought us closer together, instead…'

Jodie sunk her teeth into the muffin sending crumbs spilling on to the table. 'You've got nothing to feel guilty about. Surely he didn't want to risk putting you through all that again?'

'I'm not so sure.'

'Did he apologise?'

'No. Even when he does, he doesn't mean it. He just gets annoyed at me over something else another time.'

Jodie reached for a paper napkin to wipe her hands and swept up some of the crumbs.

'Mid-life crisis,' she stated.

'You think?' said Marion.

'Let's see. Is he being overly sensitive?'

'Oh God! He thinks everything you say about him is a criticism. He used to laugh when you teased him, now he can't take a joke any more.'

'Is he worried about losing his hair? Developing a paunch?'

'No. He has no need to worry about middle age spread. But thinking about it, he has been visiting the gym more often.' She shrugged. 'Maybe you're right.'

'So what's he got to say about all of this?' Jodie took the last bite of her muffin.

'I don't know. I've just sort of put up with it until I can't any more. It's as if the house is carpeted in egg shells. I always have to tread carefully in case I say the wrong thing.'

'Want my advice? Jodie asked. 'Never mind the small talk. You need to make a point. Show him how much his behaviour upsets you. You could put him to the test. Remember that film where she goes off to Greece because her hubby was always taking her for granted?'

'*Shirley Valentine*,' Marion added.

'Well, why don't you do that? Go on holiday without Richard. Even better, don't tell him until you're there. That should bring him to his senses.'

It was exactly the sort of thing that Marion expected Jodie to say. She always went straight for the jugular, never any messing around. Sometimes, Marion felt sorry for Kevin.

'You're wicked you are!'

'What's the worst that could happen?' Jodie exclaimed. 'My bet is, he'll run after you, begging forgiveness or he'll finally realise his mistake and mope around till you come back.'

'Or he'll happily wave me off and not bat an eye.'

'Well, if that's the case and I was you, I'd make damn sure I had a good holiday then I would find myself a solicitor when I got back.'

She reached out and gave her friend's arm a concerned squeeze. 'You have to be true to yourself Marion. If not, you'll only end up living a lie.'

Marion thought all afternoon about what Jodie had said. Was it simply middle age? At forty-four, she would not have called Richard that, and she doubted he would put himself in that category either.

She was back to feeling guilty.

Everything was her fault.

8

In room 201 of the Queens Hotel in Leeds city centre, Clare lay with her head on Richard's shoulder, running her hands through the dark brown hair on his chest. A door banged in the corridor; she could hear muffled voices and a woman's laugh.

He gave her a squeeze and kissed the top of her head.

'You need a shave,' she remarked, tracing his jaw line with her finger.

'I don't normally see you on a Saturday; you're lucky Marion is at the hairdressers. If I'd have known I was going to be cuddling up to you I'd have made an effort. But then again...'

He moved downwards gently rubbing his chin over her stomach and breasts.

'Stop it! It tickles.'

She laughed and squirmed whilst trying to push him off.

He threw her a cheeky grin and kissed her briefly on the lips before moving to sit on the edge of the bed.

Clare watched him dress. She did not take her eyes of his body. He was in good shape, her heart quickened with desire.

'Don't you have any more meetings where we can stay overnight…or even better, for the whole weekend like we did in Newcastle?'

Richard knew that had been a pure fluke. Marion was working double shifts at the hospital due to staff shortages, and one of his drivers had complained of not being well enough to make a delivery. Even though technically as Operational Director he did not carry out deliveries anymore, he had seen the perfect opportunity to get the job done and spend a whole night with Clare in the process. He doubted it would happen again.

Standing, he fastened the belt on his trousers then winked at her. 'I'll see what I can do.

She smiled. 'Are you ever going to tell Marion about us?'

He did not know whether she was joking or not. 'I have to find the right time; these things aren't easy. Soon, I promise.'

'I love you.' Clare announced.

He sat back down on the bed and leaned close to her. 'I love you too.'

'I don't like sharing you.' Clare stated. 'I wonder what Marion would do if she found out?' She cocked her head on one side in mischief. 'So are you going to tell her or shall I?'

He had never had to make any promises to Clare before. Until now, she had never asked anything from him. It unnerved him. If Marion found out …well it was all her fault anyway. He wanted her to scream, lash out, smash a few plates, even hit him if it helped. Anything to get rid of the heartache she felt over losing Anna instead of bottling it all up.

He wanted to yell, 'What about me? I'm still here.' Instead, he had turned to Clare. How easy it had been to go from a couple of innocent drinks in the pub to her bed, and now he was cheating on his wife.

Clare hugged her knees into her chest. 'Anyway, I don't understand why you would want to be with a middle-aged woman heading towards the menopause when you've got me.'

'Have you forgotten how old I am? You're having an affair with a man almost twice your age.'

'I know, but you would never tell,' she purred and patted the mattress next to her. 'Come back to bed. Your wife can wait a bit longer.'

'I wish I could. I have to go.'

Clare sighed. 'One of these days it'll be Marion you're walking out on, not me.'

He blew her a kiss, picked up his jacket from the back of the chair and left.

Clare watched him go.

She had always preferred older men; they had more experience of life. It wasn't only the sex, the conversation was more interesting: they'd done more, seen more and at Richard's age they had a well paid job and could afford hotel rooms and nice wine. Richard was the first she had fallen in love with and he was the first one to be married.

She longed for the door to re-open and for him to come back to her, not only now, this minute, but every night. She resented Marion for having that with him.

Richard would always come first in her life. She would not fail to appreciate him and would always make him happy — if he let her. There was just the problem of Marion.

If Richard did not say something to her soon, she would have to think of a way to speed things up.

9

Marion sensed the fraught atmosphere at the hairdressers as soon as she walked in. There were usually two stylists working along side the owner, Timothy, she could only see one.

   As she hung up her coat, Timothy, with a head of blond highlights, and wearing pale pink trousers and a white short-sleeved shirt, excused himself from his client and hurried over to speak to her. He had a flustered expression on his face.

   'Marion! Darling!' He bent forward to give her the cheek-to-cheek kiss he gave all his long-term customers, 'I'll be with you in a tick. Charlene has the flu and I'm all at sixes and sevens this morning. Cathy, get Marion a cup of coffee and some magazines will you, I shan't be long.'

   He returned to finish the hair of the woman he had abandoned to come and greet her.

   Cathy was a school girl with a Saturday job at the salon. She usually washed hair and cleaned up but today, because they were short of a stylist, she also had to make coffee for those customers who had to wait. She forced a smile and asked for the third time that morning, 'Milk and sugar?'

   Marion sat down in a black faux leather armchair and rifled through the pile of magazines on the glass table in front of her. She liked to read *Hello* or some other woman's magazine that was full of gossip but more and more they featured people she didn't know. A colourful magazine called *Simply French,* had been casually placed at one end of the table as if someone else had been looking at it before throwing it down. She picked it up and flicked through the pages, more interested in the photos than the articles.

She remembered her sister going to France once with her niece and nephew, and particularly remembered Alice telling her about the oysters; how they had all tried them and Jake had spat his out rolling around as if he had been poisoned! Alice had told her they were slimy, disgusting things.

She wondered if she dare she go on holiday on her own, as Jodie had suggested. Lots of women did. One of the nurses at the hospital went away for a week each year without her husband and had a damn good time by all accounts. She did not need Richard's permission, although she doubted he would be very happy when she told him, if she told him. That was the easier option; just leave. It would be much less hassle to tell him in a phone call once she was there. However, that would make her a coward and Richard even angrier than he already was with her these days. She would have to give it some careful thought.

Cathy brought the coffee as Marion reached the centre pages of the magazine. The photograph that spanned both pages was of a beach. The sky appeared the deepest of blues and in contrast, the sand was pale, deep and soft, bordered by pine trees with bent trunks and twisted branches. The photographer had captured the warmth and tranquillity of the place, so vividly that she could feel it radiate from the page. She imagined herself sprawled on the sand, her body bathed in warm sunshine, lulled to sleep by the sound of the waves as they gently caressed the beach.

In the distance, someone was talking to her.

'Are you ready to have your hair washed now?'
'Oh! Yes, I was miles away. Would you mind if I took this magazine,' she asked Cathy.

As Marion drove home, she sighed with frustration at the thought that Richard would once again be cocooned in the study working. She remembered when Saturday afternoons used to be for browsing around shops.

Richard's car was not in the drive when she reached the house. Perhaps he had gone to the football stadium, to watch Huddersfield Town play and had forgotten to tell her.

She picked up the kettle and saw a yellow post-it note stuck on the handle, peeling it off she read the message.

Got called away to the depot don't know when I'll be back.

A familiar disappointment cursed through her until she realised his absence gave her the perfect opportunity to look further at the magazine she had taken from the hairdressers. She made the tea and, with a sudden feeling of excitement, turned to the centre pages to read all about the location of the photograph. It had been taken somewhere on the South West Coast of France. The more she stared at it, the more excited she became.

. She was so engrossed in the article, she barely heard Richard's car in the drive. Hastily, she hid the magazine in one of the kitchen drawers. She did not want Richard to see it before she had decided what she was going to do.

Richard came in through the door, she thought he looked tired and felt a sudden pang of guilt for even considering a holiday whilst he appeared to be working himself too hard.

'Where have you been?'
'Didn't you read my note? There was a delivery at the depot.'

'Yes, but why do you always have to go? You look done in.'

He brushed passed her, mumbling about needing a shower and disappeared upstairs without another word.

Marion made her decision there and then.

The following evening, whilst Richard took himself off to his study with some excuse that he had to prepare for a meeting at work, she busied herself in the kitchen trying to decide how best to broach the subject of their marriage and her holiday.

She poured them both a glass of red wine, took a large gulp for some Dutch courage then took the glasses up to the study, pausing in the doorway to look at him. It was hard to believe he was the same man she had met in a bar one New Years Eve and been married to for eighteen years. Of course, he was older and his hair was beginning to thin. But it was not his looks that had changed so dramatically, it was the manner in which he spoke to her.

Richard was busy typing; he did not even acknowledge her presence. When he turned, there was a look of surprise on seeing her standing there. He quickly closed his laptop and took the wine glass from her. Without taking a drink, he placed it on the desk.

The study, a small box of a spare bedroom, had space for only one chair. Pushing aside a pile of papers, Marion perched on the end of the desk, half expecting him to kick up a fuss for having moved them.

She took another sip of wine before breathing deeply in an effort to compose herself. She did not intend for this to turn into a slanging match.

'Can we talk?'

Richard stared at his desk, toying with the stem of his wine glass. 'About what?' He did not bother to look at her.

Her heart was beating fast and she took another deep breath. 'I think it would be a good idea if we had some time apart from each other.'

He shot her a wary glance. 'Why would you think that?'

'Because it hasn't been much fun for either of us since…'

'Not that again! Must you always rake up the past? Can't you let it go?'

'You blame me don't you? For everything'

'Have I ever said I blame you?'

'You don't have to say it.' She sighed. 'I've decided to go away …on my own.'

He stared at her.

She ignored his silence and continued. 'It will give us time to think about the future.'

'Clearly it doesn't seem to matter what I think. You've obviously made up your mind even before discussing it with me.'

'Well if you don't blame me why can't you be nice to me?'

'You're so engulfed with what happened. I don't exist anymore.'

'You don't understand, do you?'

'Enlighten me. What don't I understand?'

'You simply moved on, back to your precious job. Do you know what I saw at the bus stop yesterday? I watched a pregnant woman smoking and she already had a child in a pram. I bet it never crosses your mind how unfair it is that women who smoke and drink through their pregnancy can still pop babies out with no problem. You called me a geriatric mum and said I should have rested more instead of carrying on working. I have to live with the fact that maybe you were right and I got it so wrong.'

'I didn't mean it like that. I know women have babies in their late thirties even older these days, and there is no evidence it would have made any difference if you had stopped work earlier. I was concerned, that's all. Apparently that was wrong.'

'You cared so much it felt like you were wrapping me in cotton wool. Why can't you see I need you to do that now? I can't take anymore. I have to get away.'

'You sound like my Father. He didn't come back. Do you expect me to just let you get on with it?'

She tensed. She had not envisaged he would react quite like this. The impact his father had made when he decided to leave, had not crossed her mind. At the time, it did not seem to bother Richard. Anyway, she did not intend it to be permanent. It was only for two weeks.

'Why in God's name would you think that I would let you go away on your own? What sort of husband does that?'

'One who cares about his wife and his marriage?'

'I do care.'

'Well, you have a funny way of showing it.'

She moved over to the door. She needed to have some space, some time to think, away from all of this.

'Please don't try and stop me Richard.'

10

The Cocked Hat pub on Otley Road, approximately three miles from Leeds city centre, was full most nights with groups of students from the university. The décor, fixtures and fittings were a shrine to its regulars. The original dark oak-varnished floor was almost bare in places due to numerous spillages over the years, and the landlord had tried to disguise the nicotine stains on the walls by hanging sports memorabilia and holiday postcards over the worst areas. In the larger of the two rooms, scratched wooden chairs and tables provided the opportunity to have a drink in relative comfort. Whilst the smaller room, used at the weekends by local bands, was devoid of seating except for a padded bench with a stained and torn blue velvet cover that stretched the width of the back wall underneath the window.

It was not the type of place, where a woman dressed in a short pencil skirt and a low cut blouse would normally be seen drinking. An older man dressed in a suit stood out even more. However, if you were a married man wanting to meet an attractive, younger woman without the risk of bumping into anyone you were likely to know, it was usually a safe place to hide.

Richard and Clare were once again taking advantage of Marion's late shift at the hospital. After a few drinks, they would get a takeaway and go back to her house in Headingly. He would be back in his own bed by the time Marion got home from work.

At about the same time as Richard was finishing off his pint of Tetley's, Police Constable Kevin Flannagan was parking the patrol car in the car park at the side of the pub. He and Police Constable David Trent were there to make enquiries about a serious physical assault that had occurred outside the pub on the previous Saturday evening. Two men in their early twenties, believed to be locals but not students, had been involved in a fight; both had been taken to hospital. As usual, the police suspected drugs to be the root cause and were seeking the name of a third person believed to be a dealer.

Kevin knew there was little hope of them getting it but it was their job to try. The sooner they finished, the sooner they could clock off their shift, which was supposed to end at 7 p.m. — precisely the time now.

The bar stretched along the width of the back of the largest room and was open at one end to the corridor that led from the entrance door to the toilets at the rear. Several groups of drinkers were either sat at tables or propping up the bar.

Kevin wished he had been a student away from home; out drinking most nights. They either had one hell of an overdraft or rich parents. He doubted if any of them made morning lectures. They probably surfaced about midday then worked the afternoon shift and returned to the bar before tea, which he imagined mainly consisted of takeaways. The students he had met did not know how to cook. Of course, his wife would disagree. She had studied at Leeds University before deciding on becoming a nurse. It was long before his time but he had heard the stories of the wild nights in pubs up and down Otley Road, as well as the student union bar and the twice-weekly discos on Wednesday and Saturday nights. He could just see her frequenting places like the Cocked Hat, drinking pints of cider. Funny how she couldn't even stand the smell of it these days.

The two police officers approached the bar. They kept a watchful eye on the clientele in case anyone chose to leg it at the sight of them. As there was nowhere more suitable to ask their questions, they remained at the bar with their backs to the entrance of the smaller room and to Richard as he walked past them towards the Gents.

As he passed behind them, Richard glanced at the two police officers. He recognised Kevin as the husband of Marion's best friend, Jodie. The last thing he wanted was word to get back to Marion; he would have to explain what he was doing in a grotty student pub and more to the point who was with him.

In the Gents, he washed his hands repeatedly to kill time in the hope that Kevin would have left and he could return to Clare unseen.

As PC Trent was writing up the last of his notes, Kevin took a moment to poke his head into the other room. There was only one person in there, a blonde-haired woman, about mid-twenties he surmised. He was not usually wrong when it came to guessing peoples ages, it was a skill learnt fast in his line of work. She was wearing a low cut blouse and sporting a rather nice cleavage. The navy blue woollen coat she was in the process of putting on looked rather expensive to Kevin. She was certainly no student and suspiciously, she did not belong in this type of pub. He noticed the empty pint glass on the table, lucky sod, he thought.

Having concluded their enquiries, the two PCs made their way to the exit. The sudden sound of broken glass put Kevin on alert; he had seen too many glasses and bottles deliberately smashed to provoke a fight. As he turned towards the direction of the noise, he caught sight of someone who bore a striking resemblance to Richard Fletcher, the husband of his wife's best friend, entering the room where only ten minutes earlier, he had been admiring the young blonde with the cleavage.

He had found the owner of the empty pint glass.

It was all very interesting. Since she was the sole person in that room, it was easy to jump to a conclusion but it was evidence he needed to be certain he had jumped to the right one.

The blonde had been putting her coat on when he saw her, which meant they were about to leave. He rushed Dave back to the car. 'I'll explain later,' he said.

He manoeuvred the patrol car hastily out of the car park into a side street opposite. Five minutes later, he had all the evidence he needed.

Richard and Clare emerged from the pub with their arms wrapped around each other. As they turned into the car park, Clare reached up and kissed Richard on the lips.

From his seat, Kevin could see that Richard showed no signs of resisting. Hadn't Jodie recently told him how Marion nearly broke down in the canteen because she was at the end of her tether with Richard? Here he was, seeking comfort elsewhere.

Jodie and he had never wanted children. They had two cats; Jodie's choice, as was the horse she kept at the local riding stables, at an enormous cost. He did not mind, he loved her and without kids what else would they spend their money on? It had been a joint decision not to have any, and after seeing what Marion and Richard had been through it was one Kevin had never regretted. Now Marion had a husband who was cheating on her as well.

As far as Kevin was concerned, there was only one choice to make. Jodie needed to know about this.

11

As soon as Marion had the opportunity, she retrieved the magazine from the drawer in the kitchen. Richard had said nothing further on the subject of her going away; in fact, they had avoided talking about it altogether. She contemplated whether it would have been better to have suggested marriage guidance or something, first. Maybe disappearing for a short while was not really the best way to resolve the problem between them, after all, this had been Jodie's idea, but *she* wasn't Jodie. She had never been away on her own before. There was something quite scary about it all.

   She switched on her laptop and began searching for *Chambres d'hôtes*, the French equivalent to Bed and Breakfast. A white house with pale green shutters and window ledges adorned with geranium displays caught her eye. The position of it was ideal; a short walk to the harbour and beach area in one direction, the shops and local market in the other. Her finger remained poised on the mouse as she stared at the screen. This would either make or break her marriage and there was only one way to find out. With a click, she booked herself a two-week holiday in La Palmyre on the Atlantic coast of France, in the home of Madame Véronique Dubois.

Now all she had to do was tell Richard.

*

Jodie noticed the chocolate bar on the tray and smiled.

'So, tell me,' she said. 'Have you decided what you're going to do?'

'I told him I wanted to go away on holiday on my own, just like you suggested.'

'And how did he take it?'

'Not good. He doesn't think there's a problem. Well, he does, but it's not him.'

'Now isn't that just typical of a man,' Jodie responded. 'They bury their heads in the sand and pretend nothing is wrong and, even when they acknowledge something is wrong, it's never their fault. So where have you decided to go?'

'To France for two weeks. I know! It's not a glamorous location but I've never been before. Carol has with the kids; she's always said she liked it.'

That reminded Marion, she must talk to her sister about Alice before going away.

'Besides I want to try some oysters and find out what all the fuss is about.'

'Are you sure about this?' Jodie asked.

'As sure as I'll ever be. It's too late now. I've booked everything.'

'You will be alright on your own? You know what a reputation these French men have.'

'No. But wouldn't it be nice if I was given the opportunity to find out?' Marion teased.

'Well then, *ooh la la* and all that!' Jodie laughed. 'How's your French?'

'Let me see. *Bonjour* is hello, *Merci* is thank you and *Au Revoir* is goodbye. Oh! And I can tell someone my name and ask the time, beyond that I'm stuck. I'll just have to point. I don't really care. Other people manage. It'll be an adventure; my adventure.'

*

Carol was nothing like her sister. Whilst Marion was slim, Carol had always carried extra weight around her hips. She had a short, almost boyish style hair cut, more murky brown than red like Marion's.

'Why an earth would you want to go away on your own when you've got a perfectly good husband to go with?' Carol whispered.

They were in the jeweller's shop where Carol worked. A customer was browsing the selection of gold chains, and Carol didn't want her to hear the conversation. The lady clearly took the hint that she was in the way; she left without purchasing anything.

'Now look what you've done! You're driving away my customers.'

'The only thing Richard is perfect at is chewing my ear off the minute I open my mouth. What's good about that?'

'Well I've never known you not to stand up for yourself,' Carol answered.

'It's not a case of not standing up for myself, I'm fed up with having to. I just want to go where I can relax and please only me for a while. Is that so unfair to want that?'

'No I don't suppose it is. I just hope you know what you're doing and, I hope you have a husband to come home to when you've finished enjoying yourself.'

'Unless he's a changed man, I'm more afraid I won't want to come home.'

The door opened and another customer walked in. This time, Marion pretended to be looking for something to buy. When Carol had finished gift-wrapping the customer's purchase and had said goodbye, Marion raised the subject of Alice.

'She's looking pale and tired and looks like she's lost weight. She chews her nails and she's stopped playing sport, something she used to love doing, and was damn good at it too. Her schoolwork is suffering, and she tells me she's regularly ill. What do you suppose is going on Carol?'

Carol sighed with resignation. 'That's just it. I don't know.'

'Well I do. I reckon she's being bullied.'

'Bullied! She'd say if she was.'

'Well she wouldn't admit it to me and like you said, we are pretty close.'

'Did you ask her?'

'No. I didn't get the chance. If she won't tell you anything why don't you go and speak to the teachers or what about her best friend, Suzy? Surely, she'll know what's going on.'

'I don't think they speak much these days. There doesn't seem to be the usual sleepovers or get-together at the weekend.'

'Look, if you need me to try again I will… but I'm leaving in a week.'

'You did the right thing not having children,' Carol said. 'They're nothing but a worry whatever age they are.'

Marion gave her sister a hug. 'Alice feels like she's as much my daughter as yours and your worries are my worries.'

Carol half smiled then turned away.

Marion left the shop to go home. She had yet to figure out how she was going to tell Richard.

She was chopping onions when he walked in the door.

He mumbled 'Hello.'

Mimi sensed the icy atmosphere and ran upstairs out of the way.

Marion finished preparing the lasagne and put it in the oven; she made a start on the salad.

Richard took a beer from the fridge. 'Do you want some wine?' he asked.

'Not tonight thanks.' She wanted to keep a clear head for later.

After they had eaten, Richard left her to clear away the dishes as usual whilst he settled himself in front of the television. She loaded the dishwasher, her heart pounding. When she had finished she went to join him in the living room.

He sat in the armchair; an old-fashioned high backed, winged chair, he had taken a fancy to at an auction they had gone to in Wetherby one wet Sunday. She remembered they had to sit through the duration of the auction before the chair came up for bidding. It was covered in a purple velour fabric; Richard was the only one that wanted it. He paid £20 and a further £500 to have it re-covered to match the sofa, on the end of which, Marion now positioned herself.

'I booked my holiday today.' She waited for the explosion.

'Did you?' His eyes never left the television.

'I'm leaving next week.'

He did not move or say anything in response. There were no objections, no threat of chaining her up or locking her in a room to stop her from going. Maybe he was going to wish her a nice time after all. Either that or she had been right to think he did not care about the holiday and had just pretended the other night to be against her going. Perhaps Jodie was right and this was the sign that their marriage was over, though she was not prepared to believe it.

'I'll make us some coffee.' She escaped to the kitchen where she could breathe.

When she returned to the living room, Richard had fallen asleep. She took the coffee back to the kitchen, not convinced she had heard the last from him. Something about his calmness unnerved her.

12

Marion emptied both drawers to the mahogany sideboard and left all the contents strewn over the top. Next, she emptied the files and documents from the box under the bed, leaving them spread over the floor along with the contents of her underwear drawer.

The house looked as if it had been burgled.

She was an organised person. Her passport, she knew, was always kept in the sideboard drawer in the living room; it had never been put anywhere else. She decided to phone Richard.

Richard picked up the phone after letting it ring several times. He had seen from the screen that it was Marion and cursed her under his breath for ringing on a Monday morning, the busiest time of the week, not that all days were not busy, chaotic would be a better description. Since they had needed to lay off two drivers, he was now having to do the work of three men. It was stressing him out. He had been looking forward to a cosy couple of hours with Clare over lunch; instead, he had to do a delivery to Sheffield. Clare had chewed his ear off about letting her down and not caring about her and now Marion was pestering him. If this was something to do with her idea of going on holiday… he had said all he was going to say. It was her fault she did not listen to him.

'I don't suppose you've seen my passport anywhere have you? It's always in the drawer in the sideboard with yours but it's not there. Yours is, but not mine.'

'How should I know what you've done with your passport? I'm not responsible for looking after your things. Is that all you've rung me about? Couldn't it have waited? I don't have time for this, Marion; I have a job to do. I'll see you later.'

Richard waited until the secretary left the office for something. He hated sharing with her, he was a Director for God's sake; he should have his own private space, but only Paul was allowed to have that. He preferred his operational staff to be always approachable and hands on should there be any problems. 'Only the Managing Director,' he said, 'should appear to distance himself from the employees.' Richard wondered if by distance, Paul meant the ten miles between the Golf club and the office, for that was where he could usually be found.

He retrieved the key from his brief case and unlocked the drawer to his desk. Marion's red passport was still tucked away at the back. After she had announced her intentions to go on holiday, his first feeling was of relief that the conversation had not been about Clare. His second was of anger. This was typical of Marion; everything had to be on her terms. *She* did not want another child, so they had not bothered trying. Now *she* wanted to go on holiday and he did not even get an invite to go with her because *she* wanted time on her own. His objections might have been ignored but this was far from over.

He would not let her go.

*

Marion could not believe she was the only person to have booked to go somewhere and been unable to find their passport. She was due to leave in six days; there was not enough time to apply for a new one.

Sister Harding approached her with an armful of blue files. She handed them to Marion one by one with a brief set of instructions for each patient.

'Cubicle one. Mr Macelroy needs fifteen-minute obs. There's a young girl in cubicle four with a suspected broken arm, she'll need an x-ray sorting and dear old Olivia has been brought in, another nasty fall. See if you can get hold of someone in Orthopaedics, and there's some suturing waiting for you in cubicle six.'

Marion put the pile of files down on the desk. She took the top one and began reading the notes inside.

'I heard you're off to France at the weekend,' the Sister said. 'Lucky you, it's my favourite place. I always fancied a little stone holiday cottage with blue shutters and hollyhocks growing up the walls.'

She sighed as if it was already a foregone conclusion that it would never happen. 'One day, maybe, if I win the lottery.'

Marion arranged for the young girl with the suspected broken arm to be taken to x- ray, before turning her attention to the elderly lady in the adjoining cubicle.

Dear old Olivia was aged eighty-nine and lived on her own. She was adamant she was not going into a care home.

'They won't separate me from my plants,' she told Marion the last time she was admitted, after falling down the steps in her beloved garden.

'What will I do if I don't have my plants to attend to?'

Her family were scattered far and wide, except for a son and his wife who lived a mile away. He checked on her daily but it was too much for him, all these falls, especially in the night. She was supposed to wear an alarm around her neck that alerted his mobile if she needed him but she kept forgetting to put it on. The whole family and everybody else come to that, knew she would be safer being taken in to care, but she was stubborn and determined to resist.

Marion reached for Olivia's wrist and held it, checking her pulse. 'How did it happen this time? Olivia. Not in the garden again, I hope.'

'Oh no, I was talking to the nice lady that lives opposite. The next thing I knew, I was lying on the road. I must have stepped back and lost my footing, I don't quite remember.'

'You've got a cut on the back of your head, and the paramedics said you were complaining that your hip hurt. We need to check that you haven't broken anything.'

'Oh I hope not, dear, I can't stay here. What will happen to my geraniums?'

'I'm sure no one will dare let anything happen to your geraniums or all your other plants.' Marion smiled reassuringly at her.

She adjusted the pillows to support her and looked at the back of her head. The blood had dried and congealed on her hair. Marion began cleaning it away so that she could assess the injury.

'So, you're off to France, how exciting,' Olivia said.

'How did you know?' asked Marion.

'I heard the other nurse just now.'

Marion finished examining the cut. 'It's not bleeding anymore and I don't think you need stitches, but I'll confirm with the doctor.' She peeled off her protective gloves and made Olivia more comfortable.

'Well, I should be leaving this weekend but I seem to have mislaid my passport. I'll have to cancel the holiday and apply for another one which can take weeks.'

'You can get one of those emergency things,' Olivia said. 'It happened to my son you know, someone stole his brief case. I couldn't understand why he was carrying his passport around with him in the first place, mind you. He went somewhere and they gave him a new one the same day. Don't worry dear, this sort of thing must happen all the time.'

Marion smiled with relief.

When she had the opportunity, she searched for the information on the internet she needed. Then she rang Jodie to explain her predicament and ask if she could exchange shifts with her on Thursday, so she could go to the passport office in Liverpool to sort everything out.

The bedroom light was still on when she arrived home from the hospital; it meant that Richard was still awake. Often, when she worked the late shift, the house was in darkness when she returned home, and she would tiptoe into the spare bedroom so as not to disturb him.

Richard watched his wife swap her baggy t-shirt and jeans for another baggy t-shirt and some multi coloured skintight pyjama bottoms she slept in. In the past, she would wear the silky negligees he had bought for her, the ones with the thin straps and lace edging, like those he now bought for Clare.

Marion climbed into bed. 'I still haven't found my passport, I've got to go to Liverpool now on Thursday and get another one.'

Richard made no comment, switched off his bedside lamp and settled down with his back to Marion.

The following night, despite her shift not finishing until after midnight, she found that Richard was waiting up for her again. He was sat up in bed, flicking through the pages of a sports magazine.

'You've had a phone call, some French woman,' he said.

'What did she say?'

'Something about her husband being really ill and she has had to close the *Chambres*... whatever it is. She said she'd be in touch some time but that you can't go this weekend.'

Richard's eyes never looked up from the magazine pages. He did not see the crest fallen face of his wife.

'I suppose you're glad that I can't go.'

'I didn't understand why you wanted to go in the first place so don't blame me that it hasn't worked out.'

In the darkness, Richard fell into a peaceful sleep. Marion lay awake, tears of disappointment trickling down her cheeks. Whatever she did or said seemed to be wrong. She really believed that a break from each other would help them to sort out what had come amiss with their marriage. She could not even get that right.

She woke in a bad mood. Lack of sleep had turned the disappointment into anger. She pretended to be still asleep until she was sure Richard had left for work before going downstairs, where she put milk and cereal in a bowl and fetched her laptop. Maybe Madame Dubois had sent her an e-mail to explain further what had happened and tell her she could go another time soon.

She was right, there was an e-mail from her, but it was not what she was expecting.

Dear Madame Fletcher, I am sorry to receive the e-mail that your mother is ill and you cannot come to stay. I hope you can come another time. Best wishes Véronique Dubois

What e-mail? What was she talking about? Her mother had died ten years ago from complications as a result of pneumonia. Marion had found her at the bottom of the stairs one morning when she had visited before her shift started. Her mother had lived on her own since her father's death, thankfully not far from either daughter.

She slumped back in the chair, feeling nauseous and pushed the bowl of cereal away from her. The first thought to cross her mind was that it must be a hoax; people at work were often talking about scam e-mails. Then she thought that Madame Dubois had the wrong person, someone else had cancelled and she had sent the e-mail to her by mistake. As for the phone call, Richard said he had received; she was completely at a loss. Maybe he had misunderstood her, especially with her French accent.

She typed a reply.

Dear Madame Dubois, I think there must be a mistake, I didn't send you an e-mail, maybe someone else did and you have mistakenly sent me their reply. I will be there on Saturday as arranged. Regards, Marion Fletcher.

Marion sat staring at the screen, willing Madame Dubois to reply without any delay and confirm that everything was alright. After ten minutes of flicking between the weather, her e-mails, Facebook and back to her e-mails, she got up, scraped the cereal into the bin before putting the bowl into the dishwasher. She looked at the screen; there was still no reply.

She put the pile of washing she had dumped on the kitchen floor into the machine and set it going. She looked again; there was still no reply. Adrenaline was flowing through her body, she was restless, she had to keep busy, it was going to be alright she told herself, calm down, it was a simple mistake. She forced herself upstairs to get dressed, not caring what she wore, without stopping to brush her hair, she raced back down to the kitchen.

Véronique had replied.

Dear Madame Fletcher, I received your e-mail last night. It was definitely from you. I do not understand if you did not send it but I am glad you can still come.

Marion did not understand either; she frantically tried to think of an explanation. For a start, she was at the hospital last night she could not have sent an e-mail. Richard was the only one here and... Oh God! He knew her password; she used the same one for everything. He was always reprimanding her for it but it was too confusing to have several different ones; she would forever have to reset them. She went into her sent box but there was no record of an e-mail having been sent last night.

It had to be Richard. He had never hidden the fact that he did not want her to go. If he had been responsible, he had cleverly covered his tracks and deleted anything that would link him to having done so. She had a sudden thought; had he taken her passport as well? Then when that had failed, resorted to this?

She felt in a state of shock.

She would have to talk to him, find out if she was imagining all of this, but what was he going to say? If he were guilty of all these things, he would not admit to it. Well, he would have to, and then what was she going to say to him? It was not normal behaviour for a husband. God, she had no idea what was going on with him. What she did know however, it was time she looked after herself.

She splashed her face with cold water and pulled herself together. After sending a polite reply to Véronique, apologising and once again confirming that she was still coming, she began to make plans.

Firstly, she deleted all her correspondence with Véronique. Then she printed off her flight details and the confirmation booking at the *Chambres d'hotes* and deleted them from her files.

The suitcase was stored on the top of the wardrobe, if she took it now Richard would know. She would ask Jodie if she could borrow one and collect it on her way back from Liverpool. It could stay in the boot of the car until Friday morning and then she would pack it whilst Richard was at work and keep it in the car until she left on Saturday. Richard would have no idea she was still going. She would play along with him and pretend that her holiday was cancelled. Finally, she would make some excuse about needing to go shopping and head straight for the airport.

She would consider whether to text him when she was on the plane.

*

Jodie watered the spider plant in the living room for the fourth time without realising it. All she could think about was the woman Kevin had seen Richard kiss on the lips.

'Are you going to let her find out from someone else or are you going to be honest with her?' Kevin said.

'She's my best friend. I'm sure she'd rather hear it from me.'

She stared out of the living room window, her mind in a whirl. Marion would be here any minute to collect the suitcase. How was she going to tell her?

'Has Richard told you he was in the Cocked Hat pub with another woman? Has Richard told you about the woman he's been seen kissing?' Of course he would not have told her; there was no point asking that. 'Do you know Richard has been seeing someone behind your back?'

She could just put it simply. 'Richard's having an affair.'

She tried to imagine what Marion would say or do if the roles were reversed. Marion would make sure of her facts first. She would ask Kevin outright before saying anything. That's what I'm going to do, thought Jodie. If Richard is having an affair, she would give him the chance to tell Marion or she would do it for him.

Having made the decision to put the responsibility back on to Richard, for now, she felt as if a great weight had lifted from her shoulders.

Marion arrived at Jodie's house with her new passport safely zipped inside her handbag. She knocked once before entering the door that led into the kitchen. Jodie had seen her park on the road in front of the house and was filling the kettle.

'Well? Was your trip successful?' she said, as Marion entered.

Marion patted her handbag to indicate she had the passport. 'Yes, and I'm not letting it out of my sight. Is this for me?' She pointed to the bottle green suitcase on the floor.

'I hope it's big enough,' replied Jodie.

'I don't have much I can take. It's all happened so fast I haven't had time to buy myself anything new. I hope to be wearing nothing but a bikini most days,' Marion smiled.

Jodie handed her a mug of tea and she followed her into the conservatory at the back of the lounge. It had two wicker chairs and a two-seater settee, all with navy blue cushions; it looked out over a garage and a small garden. The pale peach flowers of a climbing rose stood out against the dark brickwork of the garage wall.

'So, are you going to tell me what's going on, why the need for the suitcase and all the secrecy?' Jodie asked.

Marion cupped her hand around the mug of tea as if she was seeking warmth on a cold day, which of course it was not. The month of May had finally brought the sunshine that now streamed through the expanse of glass, making the room feel tropical. She relaxed in the warmth and told Jodie all about her suspicion that Richard had been behind her missing passport, together with the phone call and the e- mails.

'I know I should confront him. It's not that I can't, more that I don't want to. If I believe he did those things, I can satisfy myself that I'm doing the right thing in going away.'

'Why do you need to justify anything? Put yourself first for once. You're unhappy. I see that as a good reason to want to change things. Always strive to be happy, Marion.'

'You mean like you are?'

'Kevin and I understand each other; we want the same things.'

'You mean you get what you want because Kevin adores you and will do anything to please you?'

'Isn't that what every woman should have a right to? You undervalue yourself Marion. You're worth ten of Richard.'

'If I didn't know better I'd think he was having an affair with his secretary.' Marion laughed.

Jodie seethed with anger. She wanted to tell Marion that was exactly what she suspected Richard was doing.

She placed her cup down carefully on the glass table at the side of her chair. 'What does she look like… his secretary?'

'She's got short, spiky ginger hair. Richard's pet name for her is ginger nut. I'm only joking; she's a lesbian. Anyway, I always thought husbands who were playing away were overly attentive to their wives to avoid any suspicion. That rules Richard out. He can have two weeks of freedom, and what does he do? He tries to stop me from going away. Is that the behaviour of a man having an affair? Unless of course, it's all for show.'

'What would you do if he was having an affair?' Jodie said.

'Ah! The million-dollar question. The answer is, I don't know. I would want to know why before I made any rash decisions.'

Jodie decided she had been right to confront Richard before saying anything to Marion. What was best for Marion now was to enjoy sometime away. It could all be dealt with when she returned.

'When are you leaving?'

'Saturday morning. I'll tell Richard I'm going shopping, then I'll sneak off to the airport. He's left me no choice now.'

Jodie looked at Marion's pale complexion and the dark circles under her eyes.

'Make sure you have a good time, you deserve it more than you know. I'll be here if you need me.'

With the suitcase safely stored in the boot of her car, Marion headed for home to face the husband she felt she no longer knew. Only one more shift to get through tomorrow then she would be on her way to France.

She did her best that evening to act normal.

Richard, she knew, would be expecting her to be disappointed that she was not going on holiday as she had planned. She prepared the evening meal of pork chops with mashed potatoes, even making him the onion gravy he liked, and avoided speaking to him as much as she could without seeming unfriendly. Let him think he's won, she thought, he'll get a shock on Saturday.

On Friday morning, she packed the suitcase and hid it under a blanket and some old carrier bags in the boot of her car. Not that Richard would look in there, but she had to think of every eventuality now in order to stay one-step ahead of him. In order not to arouse any suspicion, all her toiletries were still in the house exactly where she would use them on a daily basis. She planned to buy everything she needed at the airport.

After her shift finished, she drove home praying the house would be in darkness, meaning Richard was asleep and she could use that as an excuse to sleep in the spare room. When she pulled into the drive, she saw with dismay that her prayers had remained unanswered, the bedroom light was still on.

Richard was wide-awake. 'I know you're upset that you can't go on your holiday tomorrow,' he said, 'so I've booked a restaurant for lunch in Harrogate. We can head off in the morning and go to *Betty's* for coffee and some of their nice cake that you like. I thought it might cheer you up.'

She slipped quickly in to her pyjamas and climbed into bed, saying nothing. She could not believe what she was hearing.

'Well? What do you think?'

She forced herself to reply, 'Fine.'

Everything was far from it.

On the way home from the hospital, *'Walking on Sunshine'* by Katrina and the Waves had been playing on the radio. She had sung along, her hands energetically tapping out the beat on the steering wheel, the words getting lost momentarily amongst thoughts of cheese and wine and lazy days on sandy beaches. Now, she was lying in bed tormented by the fact Richard wanted them to leave for Harrogate in the morning. Her own plans, that had also involved leaving in the morning but not with Richard, nor for Harrogate, were fading fast.

She could not sleep despite being tired from her shift. The light from the full moon lit up the curtains and penetrated the darkness making eerie shapes out of the bedroom furniture. Next to her she could see the outline of Richard sleeping, a good, sound sleep, while she tossed and turned, trying to make sense of why she hadn't just confronted him and demanded to know what was going on. If she had, there would not be any need for all this creeping around. It was *so* unlike him that she was scared. She would never have said he was capable of doing any of the things he had done; as far as she knew, he had not done anything like this before. Then again, this was the first time she had wanted to go away without him. With hindsight, she wished she had never told him about the holiday, she could have asked Jodie to come with her; they could have sneaked away and then phoned Richard. Although if she had done that, it was likely, he would have blamed Jodie for it all. He would not see a reason for his wife going unless she had been cajoled into it.

She thought about slashing the tyres on Richard's car or hammering a nail into them to make them go flat. They would have to take her car then, and she knew under no circumstances would he be seen in her eight-year-old, green Fiat Punto.

'It's nothing but a clapped out dustbin,' he had remarked on several occasions. 'Why don't you ever clean it?'

She knew if they could not go to Harrogate in the BMW they would not be going at all. However, to sabotage someone's tyres deliberately you needed to be vindictive, and that was not in her nature no matter how desperate she was.

Since sleep had eluded her, she slowly peeled back the covers and eased herself out of bed. If Richard were to wake up now she could not bear it. Carefully, she made her way downstairs into the kitchen, made a cup of tea and sat in the living room. According to the carriage clock on the mantelpiece, it was 3.15 a.m. It would be daylight in a couple of hours. Time was running out.

At the bottom of a pile of *Ideal Home* magazines that lay on the corner of the coffee table, Marion had hidden the travel magazine she had taken from the hairdressers. Retrieving it, she turned to the picture of the beach in the centre pages.

What was she was waiting for?

There would be no better time to escape than now, in the middle of the night, whilst Richard was asleep. It would mean that she would arrive at the airport hours early for the flight but at least she would be there, and not on her way for tea and cakes in Harrogate with Richard smirking by her side. The more she thought about it, the faster her heart beat. Could she really pull it off and get away without waking Richard up? What would she say if he caught her sneaking around in the dark?

She left the magazine on the sofa, still open at the centre pages and crept back upstairs, hardly daring to breathe. On the chair at the side of her bed were the clothes she had worn coming home from work; she could just make out the outline of them with the light from the full moon. She tiptoed slowly over to the chair. As she bent down to scoop them up, Richard turned over on to his back. She immediately dropped down onto her knees and elbows and remained there, clutching the clothes. The carpet fibres dug into her skin; her heart was racing with fear that he would wake up any minute and switch on the light wanting to know what she was doing. Closing her eyes, she pleaded, 'Please God! Please!' She realised she was holding her breath.

After what seemed like an age but in reality was probably less than a minute, she heard him begin to snore, a small part of her relaxed. Slowly, she eased herself up from her crouching position on the floor and began to breathe normally. She tiptoed out of the bedroom and went back downstairs, hastily changing out of her pyjamas in the kitchen and throwing them into the washing machine, just for somewhere to hide them.

She picked up her car keys and handbag and tentatively unlocked the kitchen door. Stepping out into the cold, dark air, she shivered then closed the door gently behind her. It felt like the stars and the moon were all watching and willing her on as she got into the car. The engine started first time and, mouthing a 'Thank you,' to God, reversed out of the drive — too quickly, forcing her to slam on the breaks to check nothing was coming. The engine stalled. She turned the key in the ignition, the car coughed and spluttered but the engine would not engage.

'Please, not now!' she cursed, remembering she had pushed the letter, reminding her that the car was due for a service, into the letter rack in the kitchen and had ignored it. She glanced up to see if the bedroom light was on and saw that everything was still in darkness. She tried to start the car again.

'Come on! Come on!' Her throat was dry and she was shaking, both signs that she was now panicking.

The bedroom light went on just as the engine roared into life.

'Oh! You little beauty,' Marion cried.

Gripping the steering wheel with both hands, she drove like a woman possessed by fear, constantly checking the rear view mirror to see if a black car was following her. She saw every red traffic light as a barrier to her escape and put her foot down hard wherever possible, desperate to put as much distance between her and Richard as quickly as she could.

She took the winding road that led her away from Huddersfield and through the pretty villages of Flockton and Bretton. As she passed the Sculpture Park at Bretton, slits of daylight were beginning to pierce the darkness; the sculptures stood out like monstrous shapes in the shadows. Just before the roundabout, which led on to the M1 motorway at junction 38, Marion pulled the car over into a lay-by and switched off the engine. She stretched her arms out in front of her to relieve the tension. Richard would have found her and the car missing by now. She hoped he wouldn't do anything stupid like phone the police. She should have left a note; it was too late now.

13

It was close to seven .a.m. when Marion arrived at East Midlands Airport. Once through the departure doors, she picked the first cafe she found that served more than just pastries and cakes; she was hungry after her ordeal, and ordered scrambled eggs on wholemeal toast and a black coffee.

She had never flown by herself before; Richard was the one who normally took charge of everything. They had always had to be at the airport in good time; he hated to be rushing anywhere, preferring to spend two hours drinking coffee in the departure lounge than risk spending it in a queue on the motorway. Marion was the exact opposite. She hated sitting around and waiting; she wanted to arrive at a place when she needed to and not before. However, this morning was an exception, she was just glad to be here.

When the check-in desk was open, she left her suitcase before wondering through the security point. Not until she strolled through the duty free shop did she finally feel herself relax, and meandered happily around the displays of perfume and make-up.

Two rows behind her on the plane a commotion had broken out. She glanced round and saw two women trying to put their luggage in the same place in the overhead locker. A rather flustered looking airhostess, with a fed up look on her face, was trying to push her way politely through the queue of people waiting to get to their seats, in order to sort out the problem. Marion was glad she had no extra hand luggage with her.

The man in the seat beside her smiled. She had been so busy watching the two women and the hostess, she hadn't noticed him arrive.

'There's never a dull moment on these flights,' he said. 'They pack us in like sardines.'

Marion smiled in agreement. As the plane taxied for takeoff, she clutched the armrest between the two of them.

'You don't look as if you like this bit,' he said.

'No, nor at the other end either.' She put her head back on the seat and closed her eyes as the plane left the ground.

The man seemed happy to chat. Marion discovered he lived in Cambridge, and was visiting his brother who had moved out to France three years previously to live in La Rochelle.

'He decided he needed to start a new life for himself after his marriage broke down,' the man told her.

'And did it work?' Marion asked.

'According to him it's the best thing he ever did. He loves living in France.'

Marion thought about Richard's father, how he had moved to live in New Zealand when Richard's mother died. She smiled inwardly; she hadn't considered that living somewhere else could be an option for her if things were not sorted between her and Richard.

Marion told him that this was her first holiday in France, if he thought it strange she was going alone, he was polite enough not to ask any probing questions. The conversation flowed between them and Marion became so engrossed she didn't notice when they were about to land. Only when they had touched down on the runaway did she have a panic-stricken look on her face, which made him laugh.

'That wasn't so bad was it?'

She eyed him suspiciously. 'You kept me talking on purpose.'

'Well it worked.' He smiled.

Marion laughed. 'I suppose it did.'

The man did not have a suitcase he needed to collect so they said their goodbye's once through passport control. His thoughtfulness had touched Marion. Richard had never cared less about her fear of takeoff or landing. Usually he would settle down with his newspaper and ignore everyone around him.

For the two weeks she was going to be in France, Marion had considered hiring a car at the airport, then decided that driving on the wrong side of the road, in a car she wasn't used to, could be a recipe for disaster. Instead, she had arranged for someone to meet her at the airport.

Monsieur Dubois, a small, rounded man with dark hair and a thick moustache, was waiting for her. He was holding a piece of white cardboard aloft with her name written in blue capital letters, she had no idea if he spoke any English. Now, she decided, would be a good time to try out her school girl French. Smiling nervously, she walked up to him and said in a quiet, apprehensive voice, *'Bonjour.'*

He smiled. 'Madame Fletcher, *bienvenue,* please my car is zis way. I take your case?'

'Thank... I mean *merci.*' Marion stuttered, somewhat relieved he could speak English of sorts.

As she stepped outside the airport building, she was met by the most vivid blue sky she had seen in a long while. Monsieur Dubois kept walking briskly towards the car park, dragging her suitcase behind him. She almost had to run to keep up with him whilst at the same time rummaging in her handbag for her sunglasses.

The journey took about an hour. The lush, green countryside passed them by, bathed in glorious sunshine. The dashboard indicated it was 25 degrees outside; Marion was thankful they had air conditioning. When she had finally arrived at the airport, she had managed to change into something more suitable for the journey than the pair of jeans and the jumper she had retrieved from the bedroom in the early hours of that morning, and was now wearing a yellow, thin-strapped top and a white skirt. The trainers, she had left the house in, had been replaced by a pair of white sandals.

Monsieur Dubois, she soon discovered, had limited English. However, like all strangers, they managed to talk about the weather. It was funny how foreigners always thought it did nothing but rain in England.

Eventually, they arrived at La Palmyre and the little white house with the pale green shutters. The picture on the internet did not do it justice. Marion thought it was delightful. To the side of the house was a stone terrace underneath a wooden pergola, the top of which was completely wrapped in the purple flowers of a wisteria plant. It provided the perfect shaded canopy for two round, green metal tables and four chairs. Red geraniums overflowed from hanging baskets and window boxes.

Madame Dubois came out to meet them and held out her hand for Marion to shake, '*Bonjour.*'

The first thing Marion noticed was her warm, generous smile. She had dark hair, swept into a neat chignon at the back of her head and was much slimmer than her husband.

Marion hesitated slightly, not used to such formalities from a woman; she shook her hand and smiled back. 'Please, call me Marion,' hoping that Madame Dubois had understood.

'And I am Véronique and my husband is Pascal.'

Her English was perfect.

Marion followed them into the house.

The entrance hall was much cooler than outside. It had a terracotta-tiled floor, and a dark wooden staircase that led off to the right. Through a door to her left, Marion could see tables laid out for breakfast the following day.

'Would you like some tea?' Véronique asked.

'Yes. Thank you,' replied Marion, realising that the last time she'd had anything to drink was at the airport and that she was parched after her journey.

'You can sit outside if you like.' Véronique pointed to a side door in the dining room that led out to the terrace area that Marion had seen when she arrived.

'You speak very good English,' Marion told her.

'My father was from Nottingham; he moved to France with his job and met my mother. He always insisted on speaking English with us from a very early age.'

'Well it's certainly paid off,' Marion remarked.

Véronique went to make the tea.

Marion wondered out on the terrace and sat at one of the tables, admiring the pendulous pale lilac flowers of the wisteria that shaded her from the hot sun. She took a deep breath and inhaled their heady perfume. Véronique and Pascal had been most welcoming. She could tell she was going to like it here. There was no one to shout at her. It was warm, sunny and picturesque, a million miles away from Huddersfield and all that had gone off there.

After she had finished her tea, Véronique took her to a bedroom on the first floor, which looked out onto a small garden at the rear of the house, the majority of which was taken up by a vegetable plot. Whatever was growing there was neatly planted up in rows. Marion laughed and pointed to the figure sat on a chair at one end of the plot. It appeared to be a man cleverly sewn from pieces of material then stuffed and dressed. A hat, with corks dangling from its rim, sat lopsided on his head.

Véronique smiled, 'I made it myself to keep the birds away.'

The room had a feeling of warmth and homeliness about it. To Marion it was typically French in that it had old oak beams and bare, dark wooden floorboards, partially covered by a patterned rug. The rest of the furniture was also of dark oak, and the walls were painted cream. Shutters replaced the need for lined curtains; instead, a pair of cream nets decorated the bare window space.

After Véronique had left, Marion unpacked quickly, eager to explore and realising she was now very hungry. She wondered out into the garden and found the Dubois' busy in their vegetable plot. Feeling obliged to let them know she was going out, she shouted 'A*u- revoir.'*

Véronique and Pascal both looked up and waved.

The guesthouse was on a long straight road. Yellow and orange rose bushes and clumps of orange poppies formed a colourful display down the centre of it, and shrubs of green and red foliage bordered the pavements.

Excited and spurred on by her empty stomach, she set off, ignoring the ringing sound that was coming from the mobile phone in her handbag.

Véronique had explained to her earlier, how she could get to the small harbour and the beach where she would find bars and cafés. At the end of the road, she turned right and in front of her was the sea, sparkling in the sunlight.

There were two bars, one on either side of the road. The one on the right, *Le Marin*, gave her a good view of the harbour and the bay beyond and looked to have the more comfortable seats, so she made a beeline for two vacant black wicker armchairs, with large padded grey cushions, and a low level smoked glass table that was positioned between them. A black umbrella provided the much-needed shade, and she was relieved to be able to take off her straw sun hat, since it was making her head sweat. Whilst she waited to be served, she watched the comings and goings of the boats over the tops of the palm plants that bordered the red asphalt terrace.

From somewhere in her bag her mobile phone beeped. Sighing, she rummaged amongst the contents of her bag to find it, and was pleased and relieved to see that the text was from Jodie, not from Richard as she expected.

'Did you escape?'

Marion had to stop herself from laughing aloud, remembering she was in a public place.

'Yes,' she typed back. 'I made it. Richard has no idea where I am.'

'Have a good time without him. Watch out for those French men!'

Marion smiled.

'*Bonjour Madame.*'

She looked up to find an attractive waiter smiling at her and holding out a menu card. She blushed and accepted the card from him, not daring to meet his gaze.

'*Merci,*' she replied and pretended to immerse herself in the white laminated list of drinks, ice creams and crepes to hide her embarrassment. She could not remember the last time a man had caused her to colour up like that just by looking at her. She settled on a Strawberry Sunday and decided that a cold beer would go down nicely.

The waiter returned.

'D*ites moi*!' he said jovially.

He had such a cheeky smile. Marion could only look away feeling uncomfortable; she had no idea what he had just said.

Sensing her embarrassment, he asked more softly in English, 'What would you like?'

His smile became warmer, less for show. Marion's stomach somersaulted as he continued to look at her. He was around her age, maybe slightly older, his dark hair was receding at the sides a little and his chin was shadowed with stubble.

She smiled back with relief and gratitude that he had chosen to speak to her so she could understand

85

After she placed her order, Marion relaxed and surveyed what was around her. Beyond the large stone boulders that made up the harbour wall, she could see a long stretch of land, partially covered in green vegetation except at the end, where there was a beach of bare, golden sand. The land resembled an over stretched, bent arm, with the sea settling in its crook forming a sheltered bay where the odd windsurfer and jet ski were spending their time going backwards and forwards.

It was impossible to see the beach and the sea on the opposite side of the stretch of land. Marion was not aware that here the turbulent waters of the Atlantic bubbled like boiling water in a cauldron. The underlying currents produced waves in all directions that crashed into one another leaving behind a wall of white spray as they tumbled forwards covering the sand in white foam.

She would experience the wild coast— *La Côte Sauvage,* another day.

At the side of the bar, Marion noticed a sailing and windsurfing school, a small car park served them both. At the far end, a path led into the pine forest, Marion assumed that this was where most people went to get their daily exercise, judging by the number of cyclists and joggers that had passed her in the short time she had been sitting there.

The waiter returned with her ice cream and beer.

'Enjoy,' he said, then smiled.

She did exactly that, relishing the time away she so desperately needed. She still could not believe she had had to sneak out of the house just to be able to be here. She was determined not to waste a second of it.

After paying the bill, and unsure whether it was customary or not, she left a fifty cent piece on the table next to her beer glass. Curious, she then followed the path into the forest and walked for a couple of minutes until she saw an opening off to her left and smiled with satisfaction at what she had stumbled upon. There, in front of her, was the exact same picture she had been looking at these past few weeks in the magazine. She could even work out exactly where the photographer had stood to take it. She took off her sandals and sunk her feet into the thick, soft sand, then made her way down to the sea and let the cold Atlantic run over them up to her ankles. Once was enough, the icy water stabbed at her flesh like pins. She could see that the beach stretched for miles and only a few bodies littered the part where she stood. It was practically empty and very peaceful, with the exception of the seagulls that flew here and there, piercing the silence with their call.

She glanced at her watch and saw it was close to 4 p.m. The sun was starting to descend low over the sea, creating a haze, and a lone yacht was working its way along the shoreline back to the harbour. If she had brought her towel she might have happily fallen asleep on the beach, after all, she had been up most of the night and it was beginning to take effect.

Véronique had told her, she would be happy to prepare a light meal in the evening whenever she wanted one. The temptation to do just that and get an early night was hard to resist. However, she was on holiday and that meant going out to sample the local cuisine. She wondered what Richard would be eating tonight; hopefully, one of those microwave meals he hated so much.

14

Sunday was market day. For the sixth time that morning, Marion had pressed *call end* on her phone without answering it.

Why couldn't Richard just leave her alone? She did not want to speak to him and have her holiday ruined just yet.

The tarmac space that served as a car park for the shops and restaurants any other day of the week was today playing host to rows and rows of colourful stalls, selling everything from food to jewellery; tablecloths to bed linen, shoes, clothes, plants and not forgetting the local wine.

Sounds of: *pardon, excuse moi,* rang out around the crowds as people tried to manoeuvre between the different stalls. The locals who frequented the market every weekend knew exactly what they had come for, and queues were forming around those selling bread, shellfish and cheese. The delightful smell of roast chicken permeated the air, reminding Marion of Sunday lunches at home.

Desperately trying to get closer to see what the stalls had to offer, she jostled shoulder to shoulder with all kinds of people. There was plenty of pretty jewellery to choose from for Alice, whilst she thought Jodie would appreciate something more alcoholic. She had tried the local aperitif called *Pineau,* last night at the restaurant, on the recommendation of the waitress; it had tasted rather like sherry, smooth, but not without a kick. She had loved it and she knew Jodie would too.

All of a sudden, there was a lot of shouting in French as a big black dog was being shooed away after having cocked its leg on one of the plants that was for sale at the edge of the car park. Marion smiled at the commotion it caused, before turning her attention back to the cheese stall she had just come across. Whilst she sidestepped a large French man in order to get a better look at the selection, her phone rang yet again.

Right, I'm switching this off, she decided, then noticed it wasn't Richard this time but Carol. She spotted a small space at the end of a row of stalls, and squeezed into it so she would not be in the way of anyone. There was nothing more annoying, she felt, than trying to get past someone who was deep in conversation on a mobile phone to the point where they just ignored everyone around them.

'Hi! Carol.'

'Don't hi me! As if you don't know why I'm calling.'

Marion was taken aback by the prickliness in her sister's voice. 'Well actually, I thought you were calling about Alice, is she all right?'

There was a pause on the other end before Carol replied. 'Why shouldn't she be all right?'

Marion ignored carol's defensiveness and continued.

'Has she said anything more about school?'

'No. I know what you think Marion, but she probably just needs some extra tuition that's all.'

Marion read between the lines. What Carol really meant was, stay out of this, she's my daughter not yours and I'll deal with it.

'So what did you call me for if not about Alice?'

'Richard keeps calling me. He's demanding to know where you are. Where are you by the way?'

'I'll only tell you if you promise you won't tell him.'

'Ok. I promise,' Carol said begrudgingly. 'I just want him to stop pestering me.'

'I'm in France, a little coastal town called La Palmyre.'

'So you did it then?'

Amused, Marion half laughed. 'Yes I did it. I'm here on my own for two weeks.'

'Well the least you could do is speak to him for all our sakes. I don't know why you don't.'

'It's complicated,' Marion sighed.

A family of four passed by, they all turned to look at Marion, suspecting that they understood English she began to feel uncomfortable and lowered her voice. 'I can't talk about it right now. I just want to get on and enjoy taking a break from Richard and everything.'

'Oh! So I'll tell him that shall I?'

'You can if you want, you won't be telling him anything he doesn't already know.'

'I suppose you understand what you're doing,' sighed Carol. 'For the life of me, I don't.'

'Look I have to go. I'll come and explain when I get back.' At least she did not have to keep her phone switched on now. She was sure there was no likelihood of Carol wanting to speak to her again in a hurry.

The call had no sooner ended when the phone beeped with a text from Richard. Exasperated with him for involving Carol in all of this, Marion thought it best to open it. She did not want him to start dragging other people into their problems, even though she had. In her opinion, he had left her no choice. If he had not put up such an objection to her coming here, she would not have had the need to involve anyone else. Perhaps by refusing to answer his calls, she had not left him a choice either.

She read the text. 'Please, please, please ring me. I'm going out of my mind with worry.'

Ha! Worry over having been found out and what I'm going to do about it, she thought. Well he could go on agonising for a while longer; she was going to buy herself something for lunch, then find somewhere to eat it first.

The blue, cloudless sky had enticed all the locals to come in to town for the morning. Every street café and restaurant was overflowing with people; there were no vacant tables to be found anywhere.

Armed with her baguette, a wedge of *Cantal* cheese, she had purchased at the market, along with a couple of tomatoes, Marion set off for the harbour and beach area where she hoped it would be less crowded.

The tide was out, a long way out, leaving behind individual lakes of shallow seawater on the exposed sand. Squeals of delight filled the air, from children who found it a source of amusement to take a long run up to a lake and then splash their way through it emerging at the opposite side.

She found a spot on the beach with a rock for a backrest, and spent the next half an hour watching the children play, whilst munching her way through the bread, cheese, and tomatoes, all the while thinking about whether she should speak to Richard or text him. Either way she had no idea what she was going to say. Had she made a complete mess of this? Should she have heeded Carol's advice and just talked to him?

The trouble was, she had tried countless times, it had made no difference. Coming to France was the only thing she could think of to make him take notice of how miserable he was making her.

The phone had remained at the side of her, silent all through lunch. Her thumb hovered over the number 1 on the key pad, the speed dial number for Richard's mobile. A seagull squawked above her head. She imagined it was saying 'Don't do it.' She could not ring him because she was not ready to speak to him. She needed more time. Instead, she typed 'Stop worrying I'm fine.' Then she pressed the send button, before she could change her mind again. Either the text would be enough to silence Richard until she got home, or having finally acknowledged him, he would now begin a deluge of further messages.

She would just have to wait and see which.

The sun was now hovering over the sea, exposing the beach to a frontal attack of intense heat from which there was nowhere to hide. Tempted by the thought of a cold beer under the shade of an umbrella, Marion shook the sand from her blue beach towel and pushed it into her bag, then headed off to the bar she had found yesterday.

The same two wicker chairs were unoccupied. She glanced around but could not see the attractive waiter. As if to confirm her thoughts that he might not be working today, a young woman came to take her order, just as the first of Richard's text messages appeared on her phone.

'I'm sorry.'

Marion imagined him in his car or at his desk deliberating exactly what to say. Frankly, she was disappointed that was all he could come up with; she had heard the words more times than she cared to remember. It was not good enough. He needed to do better than that.

She placed the phone back into her bag without replying and turned her attention to enjoying her drink and watching the events down in the harbour. A catamaran had just arrived in from the bay and was slowly making its way into a mooring. It was considerably larger than the other boats already there and manoeuvring it was proving difficult. Marion watched with fascination at the precision of it all.

When she arrived back at the guesthouse, peals of laughter greeted her as she strolled up the drive. Pascal and Véronique were sat on the terrace enjoying a drink with someone. From the back, Marion could see he was dark haired and broad shouldered. Véronique raised her hand and waved Marion over. 'Come and meet my cousin, François. He's been helping Pascal in the garden.'

The man turned around and Marion felt herself blush. François was the attractive waiter she had seen at the bar.

He smiled. *'Bonjour,'* and nodded his head to her, 'we meet again.'

He satisfied the quizzical look from Véronique by explaining how he had been the one to serve Marion yesterday. His dark brown eyes stared intently at Marion. 'Would you like to join us?

'No, but thank you,' she managed to reply. Her heart beat faster. 'I've just had a drink at the bar.'

'I'm sorry I missed you,' François said. 'I hope you'll stop by again soon.' His eyes never left her face and he smiled that broad, warm smile that had melted her the day before.

Lost for words and feeling embarrassed, Marion muster a polite smile in return, then escaped into the guesthouse.

Although Pascal was not very good at speaking or understanding English, there was nothing wrong with his eyesight. After Marion had left them on the terrace he said, 'She's sad that English woman, she shouldn't be alone, it didn't make sense. What she needs is to meet a French man that would put a smile on her face and in those pretty, green eyes. We know how to treat a woman. Eh François?'

Véronique raised an eyebrow at him as if to say, 'Is that so?'

Up in her room Marion dropped her bag and sun hat on the floor and flopped down on the bed. Why had her heart felt like it had been about to leap out of her chest, just because François had been friendly towards her — no more than that, she had felt he had openly flirted with her. Then again, that was exactly what she would expect from a French man, their reputation preceded them. He was probably married and at the end of the day, it was all harmless, it would mean nothing to him. He could not imagine how much it meant to Marion right now.

She wondered if Richard was nicer to other women than he was to her and if he meant it.

15

Richard rolled away from Clare, sat up and swung his legs over the side of the bed.

'What's wrong?' Clare said.

She moved to sit behind him, draped her arms around his neck and began planting tiny kisses on his shoulders. Irritated, he shrugged her away from him; she had to throw her arms down on to the bed to stop herself from falling backwards. A sick, churning feeling took over her stomach.

He reached down to pick up his boxer shorts from the floor and pulled them on. Pushing his hands through his hair, he sighed, sat back down on the bed and turned to face her.

She stared at him, her eyes searching his face. She was scared.

'It's over between us,' he said.

'But you love me.' Her voice was barely a whisper. 'You said it when we were at the hotel. I don't understand.'

He paused and looked away. 'I guess we all say things at times we don't mean.'

'And you didn't mean it, any of it… telling Marion? Leaving her for me?'

He shook his head. 'I'm sorry.'

'Why? Why now?' she demanded.

Richard knew this day would come, when it would be over between them. He had no idea how it would end he just knew it would. He never imagined however, the circumstances that he now found himself. Marion had gone away, without him, for the first time in their marriage. He had not wanted her to go and now she would not answer any of his calls.

When she had told him about her trip, it had scared him into thinking she might actually leave him and demand a divorce or even worse move to France permanently. Starting a new life abroad seemed to be the trend these days. He had to try to stop her from going; she must have found out what he had done. Why else would she go to such lengths to get away from him?

He had been a bloody fool, a selfish bastard. At this very moment, no one could hate him more than he hated himself. How much arrogance did it take to ignore the suffering his wife was going through and care only about promotion, a swanky new car and having a woman half his age drool all over him? He cared for Clare, but she was no match for Marion. He felt wretched.

'I'm sorry,' he said again.

'Will you stop saying that, it's not what I want to hear.' She pulled the duvet up to her chin. The tears were beginning to sting her eyes. He was not going to have the satisfaction of seeing her upset; she bit her lip to distract herself from crying.

Richard pulled on his jeans and shirt.

'So that's it?' She demanded.

'I never promised you anything,' he said as he finished fastening the buttons on his shirt.

She glared at him. 'Get out! Just get out!'

He hastily picked up his socks and shoes but did not bother trying to put them on, he felt it was best for them both if he made a quick exit.

'Bastard!' she screamed after him.

He had hurt both Clare and Marion. He thought 'bastard' was quite tame.

He closed the door to the house, although he did not expect her to be in the window watching him, he glanced up anyway as a sort of final goodbye before driving away, having already decided what he was going to do next.

16

The following afternoon, when Marion left the beach, she considered having a drink at the bar on the opposite side of the road to *Le Marin*. It was not because she wanted a change, more that she wanted to avoid turning pink when François came to talk to her. There were, however, disadvantages to doing this. The seats were not as comfortable, and the view was of the car park rather than the harbour. She also did not want to appear rude, especially since he was Véronique's cousin. So once again, she found herself at François' bar

    François watched Marion stroll slowly from the direction of the beach and hesitate. She appeared to be deciding where to go. He willed her to choose *Le Marin*; there was something about this English lady that intrigued him. He enjoyed the friendly banter with other women he served, but there was no desire to get to know what was beyond the first page. Despite being single again — he had split from his wife acrimoniously a year ago, the other women did not interest him like Marion. He was unable to put his finger on why he wanted to get to know her better, other than he knew he would find it gratifying if he could be the one to put a smile back on her pretty face.

To Marion's relief, the young girl, who had served her before, came to take her order. She sipped her beer and played the game of 'people watch'. Jodie had named it that. It involved watching other people and commenting on what they were doing or wearing. It was childish really, but good fun. She could not take her eyes of a young man sat a few tables in front of her. He wore a flat cap and was reading a book. On the table was an espresso coffee cup and a glass of water. He fascinated Marion. A young man, dressed like that and sat alone in a café, reading, belonged in Paris, not here in a small seaside town. She would ask Véronique about him, purely out of curiosity.

As Marion finished her drink, she had the feeling that someone was watching *her*. She looked around and saw François staring in her direction. He caught her eye and acknowledged her with a nod of his head before coming over to her table.

Marion felt her heart start pounding again.

'*Bonjour*,' he smiled. 'It is another beautiful day.'

It was half past four, the sun was over the sea shining directly on to the bar terrace. Relief from the heat came occasionally from the odd cloud that past across it. Marion had on a cream thin-strapped t-shirt and a navy blue cotton skirt.

'I didn't expect it to be this hot,' she said.

'Normally it's not. We are having what you English call a heat wave, *le chaleur*.'

He looked at her bare shoulders already slightly pink. 'Be carefully,' he said sincerely.

She asked for the bill before he could engage her in any more conversation.

He returned a few minutes later, and placed a black plastic bill clip on the table. '*Voila!*' he said then turned to take the order of the people sat behind her.

As she eased the receipt out from under the clip, she noticed another piece of paper tucked behind. This one had a torn edge, as if it had been ripped hastily from something. The words, 'May I see you this evening?' were scrawled in blue biro.

It could not be meant for her. She would have to tell François that he had left it at the wrong table. She waited for him to realise and hurry back to retrieve it. Whilst she waited, she reached into her purse and searched for the coins needed to pay. In her mind, she recalled how friendly François had been the day she met him at the guesthouse. How she had considered he had flirted with her. Suppose he had written the note. Her stomach lurched; she ignored it. French men, she knew, had a reputation for their mistresses, he was probably just after another notch on his bedpost and wrote notes to every lone woman he took a fancy to. Well, she did not intend to be just another conquest. The question was, why her? She was long past thinking that other men could find her attractive. Perhaps her red hair and pale skin made her stand out. Most French women, she had noticed, had dark hair and olive skin and, of course, there was the obvious fact that she was on her own.

She caught him looking at her again and found herself staring straight into his eyes; they were like pools of rich chocolate. Her stomach lurched for the second time and she could feel her cheeks burning. She hastily looked away, out towards the sea, trying to gather her thoughts. What if she made it clear to him she would only have one drink. He was, after all, Véronique's cousin; surely, he would not do anything inappropriate that might upset her guest? It would be like going out with the male nurses and doctors at the hospital, nothing different and it would not mean anything.

She delved into her bag for a pen. After a further few moments of deliberation, she wrote, 'Yes' on the bottom of the message then had second thoughts and immediately scribbled over it.

Why did she suddenly feel sixteen again? This was ridiculous! What was it Jodie had said? 'Beware of French men.' Well, Jodie had solid, reliable Kevin whilst she, on the other hand, had Richard. Taking a deep breath she re-wrote, 'Yes' under her previous scribbling out and waited for him to return to her for the money.

François approached the table looking sheepish. Marion had swapped the coins for a five euro note and tucked the piece of paper behind it. She noticed the corners of his mouth turn up slightly as he read the note before walking away without saying anything.

Now what was she expected to do? Had it all been a joke or a dare that she had fallen for? What *had* she been thinking? She stood up, desperate to leave. At that moment, François returned. Wearing a huge smile, he placed her change and the folded note on the table before picking up her empty glass and leaving. She smoothed out the paper to find that under her reply he had written, 'The harbour at 7 o'clock.'

She had two and a half hours to get back to the guesthouse and decide what she was going to wear.

Marion laid out the contents of her sparse wardrobe on the bed. There was a plain, bottle green dress; she had not worn for three years. The last time was at a friends wedding. She had bought it especially and never worn it since. Richard had said it brought the best out of her emerald eyes. Next to it, lay a cream sundress with thin straps and orange and yellow swirls.

'I've brought you one of Alice's dresses,' Carol had said one evening. 'She doesn't wear it anymore; it's too big!'

'But I'm twice her size!'

'Not now, your not. Have you seen yourself lately? I'd say you're definitely a size ten and that's without trying. You make me sick. I can't get below a fourteen.'

'Alice is seventeen and I'm forty. Ever heard of mutton dressed as lamb?'

'Rubbish! It's time you wore something more vibrant instead of those dowdy plain colours you always choose.'

'Plain and simple is my motto,' Marion said.

She had put it in the case anyway to appease Carol; it was not as if she had no space for it.

The rest of her clothes consisted of several plain t-shirts with straps or short sleeves, three cotton skirts and four pairs of shorts, the sort of thing she wore to go to the beach or to go shopping. Nothing seemed suitable for an evening out with François.

In the end, she chose the green dress and fastened a small, gold necklace with the letter M, around her neck; a short necklace was more modest than a long one. It had been a while since she had cared enough to use any make-up, so she gingerly combed a small amount of mascara onto her upper lashes and drew a pale peach lipstick hastily over her lips, enough to leave a trace of colour. She left her hair to flow loose over her shoulders instead of tied back or taken up as she normally wore it, and sparingly applied her favourite perfume, *L'Air du temps*.

When she surveyed herself in the mirror, fixed to the inside of the wardrobe door, she felt satisfied. She looked like she had made an effort, nothing too showy; she was not out to impress François. She pulled on her kitten heel black sandals and lifted a black cardigan from a hanger in the wardrobe.

No one was around when she ventured downstairs, trying desperately to stop her sandals from making a noise on the wooden steps. She felt relieved. She had not relished the prospect of having to explain to Véronique that she was spending the evening with her cousin.

From behind the lighthouse at the crook of the bay, the sun continued to shine, but with much less intensity than earlier in the afternoon. Marion was glad she had brought a cardigan; she imagined it would get cooler as the evening progressed.

At exactly 7 o'clock, she sat on one of the wooden benches overlooking the harbour. There was no activity amongst the boats, anyone who had been out sailing for the day had presumably returned by now. A middle-aged couple, her arm linked in his, strolled past with a King Charles spaniel on a lead. The woman pulled on the man's arm to hurry him along as he gave Marion a lingering look.

She checked her watch several times; François was late. She felt self-conscious alone, all dressed up but going nowhere. After ten minutes, she came to the decision that he had made a fool of her. He was not coming after all. God she had been so stupid! She would go back to the guesthouse and ask Véronique to make her some supper so she could spend the evening in her room and she would avoid going to the same bar again.

Then, she caught sight of him approaching and breathed a sigh of relief. At least, he had not stood her up. He was wearing a smart pair of jeans and a white shirt; over his shoulder, he had slung a blue jacket. She was able to get a better look at him than at the bar and realised he was quite muscular. However, his lateness had heightened the doubts she had about what she was doing there. It was a mistake and she was going to have to tell him.

When he reached the bench, he broke into a broad smile. Slowly, she got up to greet him, unsure of herself.

'*Bonsoir*,' he murmured, leaning forward to give her *une bise*, the customary French kiss on the cheek.

'*Bonsoir*.' She was so nervous that her voice was almost a whisper.

She waited for him to apologise for not meeting her as arranged at 7 o'clock, but he said nothing. Obviously, it was not important to him to be on time, nor to express any regret for his lateness.

I've been waiting here for ten minutes; you could at least say something, she thought. Perhaps now would be the time to tell him she was a married woman, albeit unhappily, and she should not be going out with a strange man she had met in a bar, no matter how attractive he was.

'I ….' she began.

He was looking at her intently. 'You have the most beautiful eyes,' he said.

She blushed. Damn it! Why did she feel like she was a schoolgirl on her first date? She forgot all about his impoliteness.

'I know of a bar on the beach at St Palais. Would you like to go there for a drink?'

Marion took a deep breath. 'Yes, I'd like that,' she said, noticing the relief behind his smile.

He set off towards the car park. Marion followed wondering which one was his car. She hoped it was not too flashy, thinking of Richard's BMW.

François stopped at the side of a red scooter, handed her a helmet and smiled.

'By the shocked look on your face, I'm guessing you weren't expecting this?'

'Not really. I've never ridden a scooter before.'

'Well then, we're going to have some fun!' He fastened the strap of the helmet under her chin.

She put on the cardigan then accepted the offer of his hand to steady herself as she climbed on, thankful that the skirt of her dress was flared enough to enable her to straddle the seat behind him not too ungainly.

'It doesn't go very fast but you need to hold on!' he shouted.

Taking that as her queue, she tentatively placed her hands on his hips. As the scooter accelerated, she whooped with a mixture of fear and excitement. Her arms sought the safety of his waist; she wrapped them tight around him, breathing in his cologne at the same time. The rush of air chilled her bare legs; she wished she was more appropriately dressed.

The coast road took them high onto a headland where the view of the bay was breathtaking. When they arrived in St Palais, Marion got off the scooter to find her legs would not work. She had sat in one position for fifteen minutes, afraid and tense.

François laughed. 'You'll get used to it — I hope.'

He was doing it again, staring into her eyes, as if her legs were not weak enough.

The bar was on a terrace overlooking a small sandy cove, lined on either side by rocks.

François placed his hand lightly on the small of her back, sending shivers up her spine. He steered her to a table at the front of the terrace, on the edge of the beach. Here, they could sit, looking out at the calm ocean, watching the gentle waves that tickled the sand. To their right, the sun was slowly sinking; soon it would disappear behind the houses higher up on the cliff top.

François ordered a beer for himself; Marion asked for a red wine.

'So, did you like your first time on a scooter?'

'My legs were cold, you should have warned me, I would have worn trousers.'

'Your dress looks beautiful on you.'

She took a large sip of wine and smiled, not used to compliments. As she looked around, she was reminded of the many holidays, when she and Richard had sat, over looking beaches whilst the sunset.

François broke the silence. 'Tell me about yourself. You wear a wedding ring, yet you are here on your own and you look sad.'

'More angry than sad,' she revealed. 'Do you mind if we don't talk about it. I'm here to get away from all that for a while. Tell me about yourself instead.'

He leant forward and rested his arms on the table; his hands toyed with his beer glass. 'What would you like to know?'

'Okay, you aren't wearing a wedding ring; does that mean you're not married?'

He looked at his ring finger. 'I was. She left me for another man and I don't really want to talk about it either.' He laughed, 'We're not getting off to a good start talking about our failed relationships. I'm certain there are a lot more interesting things we can talk about.'

She learnt that he was forty-seven, had been a headwaiter at the bar for ten years and aspired to be the owner himself one day. Occasionally, he stumbled and reverted to French before stopping and laughing when he saw her blank expression. He told her about his son who was the same age as Alice, and that he had made the effort to have English lessons to help with his job. 'And of course it comes in useful with the English ladies!' he said mockingly.

For some reason, Marion felt annoyed at his frivolous comment; she looked away, down the beach. It sounded to her like he made a habit of asking English women to spend an evening with him. She was no exception, but why should she be?

'I'm sorry,' he said. 'That was a stupid thing to say. I was joking. I don't get the opportunity very often to have a conversation like this. I didn't mean to make light of it.'

She smiled; maybe she had been too quick to judge him. In return, she told him about her job as a nurse and that this was her first time in France. Carol and Alice came into the conversation briefly but she was careful to omit anything about her life with Richard.

As darkness descended, they headed back to La Palmyre, her arms automatically seeking out his waist this time as she climbed onto the back of the scooter. At the guesthouse, he took hold of her hand and held it to his lips.

The sensation of his touch caused even the remotest parts of her body to tingle.

'Will you come to the bar again tomorrow?' he asked.

Marion nodded.

'*À demain,*' he whispered. 'Until tomorrow.'

She watched him drive away with mixed emotions. Everything about the evening had been enjoyable — apart from the scooter, yet she would have to be careful not give out the wrong signals.

17

'I love you.'

Marion had not heard those words from Richard in a long time. So long in fact, she could be forgiven for thinking someone else was writing the text message on his behalf, however, it was an improvement on the last one he had sent her; so what now?

Last night with François, she had felt like she was living in another world. Yet momentarily she had wished it had been Richard who was with her. There was a time when they had shared sunsets and romantic evenings seated at restaurant tables on the beach, now it felt like he would run a mile rather than be nice to her. So where were these sentiments of love suddenly coming from? There was no way she was going back to living the life she had with him before she came to France. She needed more proof that things would change for the better.

'Did you hide my passport?'

Richard was swift to reply. 'So, you'll only speak to me by text. This is stupid. Why won't you answer my calls and speak to me properly?'

Marion refused to be drawn into an argument. That was the good thing about texts; Richard could not shout at her.

'What about my passport?'

'I didn't hide it, I picked it up by mistake and didn't realise. It's back in the drawer.'

She wanted to believe him. It was perfectly feasible that had happened. After all, she knew someone who took her daughter's passport by mistake and never thought to look until she got to the airport.

If I'm wrong about the passport, thought Marion, let's see what he has to say regarding the phone call. Supposedly, Véronique needed to close the guesthouse when she was due to stay there because Pascal was ill. In addition, there was the e-mail he sent to Véronique.

Véronique had not mentioned the e-mails; the misunderstanding between them had been resolved. Marion was too embarrassed to bring it up, and Véronique was too polite to refer to them.

'Why did you lie about the phone call?'

The response obviously took more careful thought on Richard's behalf, since it was not instant as before. Marion stared out of the window of her room while she waited. Pascal was in the garden; his portly figure making hard work of picking green beans, lovingly cultivated and cared for by him and Véronique. It was another cloudless day; he stopped to wipe his brow with a handkerchief taken from the pocket of his shorts. There was no François to help him this morning.

Marion hung around for a further five minutes before deciding the day would not wait for Richard. She fastened the strap of her white sandals, picked up the bag with everything she would need, retrieved her sun hat from the bed and went downstairs.

Pascal was coming in from the garden, breathing heavily, small beads of sweat breaking out on his forehead. He took out his handkerchief once more to mop them up. Marion smiled and wished him a polite 'B*onjour.*'

In his discomfort, he threw her a faint smile. *'Fait chaud,'* he wheezed, continuing to dab the sweat from his brow. He pointed to the hat in her hand and nodded vigorously. *'Vous avez besoin d'un chapeau adjourd hui,'* and with that, he carried his pot of beans into the kitchen. They were the first of the season. Véronique would turn them into a mouth-watering accompaniment just the way he liked them, nice and soft, usually with some garlic and a little olive oil. They would go nicely with *Côte du porc* and some sautéed potatoes later for his lunch.

Marion made her way down the Boulevard des Régates. The sky was a vivid blue and the sun fiery. Pascal was right about needing a hat, being fair skinned she always had to be careful. She had smothered her skin in sun cream; it smelt of coconut.

It was late morning with no sign of a breeze; the canopy of pine trees in the forest would provide cool shade from the already soaring temperature. As she strolled towards the harbour, her heart was full of mixed emotions. She smiled, recalling the softness of François kiss on her hand and shuddered with joy when she thought of the way his dark eyes had appraised her face. She had none of those things with Richard. These days, she doubted he would even notice if she grew an extra head. Her heart felt heavy, her mobile phone remained silent, deepening her mood. Why was it always the case when you were not looking for something …? She was here to try to mend her marriage that was all. She was not here to have an affair and finish it for good.

The entrance into the forest began behind the bar. By the time she had reached it, her mouth was dry. She stopped and deliberated. She knew François was expecting to see her. Their evening had been a one off, exciting and enjoyable, nevertheless, it had been a one-night stand of sorts. She decided it would be best all round if she did not go to the bar, instead, she reached inside her bag for the bottle of water and drank in earnest. She would pass the day with a pleasant stroll to the lighthouse further up the coast, maybe take to the beach for a while with her book and wait to see what Richard had to say for himself.

The lighthouse, *La Coubre,* was five kilometres from La Palmyre. Marion estimated it would take her around an hour to get there. She was joined on the path by other-would be walkers and energetic cyclists. When she finally reached the giant red and white structure, she had no desire to climb its three hundred steps, despite knowing that the view from the top would be spectacular. Instead, she carried on through the forest, climbing up the sand dune that led to the beach. Her bare feet sank into the soft sand with every step.

At the top, a welcome breeze came off the sea, cooling her skin. She removed her sun hat and let the wind blow back the hair from her face. A thunderous sound came from the fierce, white crested waves, pounding the golden sand as far as the eye could see. On their backs, small figures in black wet suits clung to surf boards.

She took her place on the beach, spread out her towel, strolled down to the sea edge and stood, letting the last of the white foamed wave run over her feet. After kicking her way through the surf for a while, she returned to her towel and settled down to read her book.

By early afternoon, she still had not received Richard's explanation about the phone call; her suspicion that he lied to her grew stronger. Disheartened, she made her way back through the forest.

Close to La Palmyre, she came across a small stall selling ice cream and drinks. She treated herself to a double chocolate magnum before venturing onto the part of the beach she had come to call *her* beach, the one she had seen in the magazine. Walking down to the water's edge, she stood and let the sea cool her hot, tired feet. The magnum melted quickly in the heat; the chocolate ice cream dripped down the wooden stick. She rinsed her sticky fingers in the sea.

Out in the bay, the water shimmered in the sunlight. Windsurfers twisted and turned as if dancing on its surface. A group of boats with half-white and half-orange sails coursed up and down its length with the occasional small speedboat cutting in and around them. Closer to the shore, a couple wobbled on seaboards, attempting to paddle their way back to the beach. As it was more sheltered at this part of the coast, it felt even hotter. The limited breeze could have come from a hot air blower.

Marion felt happy and relaxed. It was a tranquil place from which to hide from the chaos of her marriage.

Back at the guesthouse, Véronique busily fed oranges through the juicer. A citrus aroma percolated the air. She stopped the machine in time to hear the front door open. Poking her head out from the kitchen, she saw Marion in the hall, her face red from sunburn or exertion.

'Fancy some fresh juice? I'll throw in some ice cubes, you look like you need cooling down,' she shouted.

'My idea of heaven!' Marion replied, appreciatively.

They took their drinks out onto the shaded terrace. Above their heads, the flowers of the wisteria were starting to fade to a pale lilac. The red geraniums, which spilled over the edge of hanging baskets and terracotta pots, now took centre stage.

Marion was so thirsty after her walk back from the beach that she almost drained her glass in one.

'So, how was your night out with my cousin?' Véronique said unexpectedly.

'You mean François?' Just the mention of his name made Marion's stomach lurch. 'Has he told you all about it?' She asked coyly.

'No.' Véronique said.

'Then how did you know?'

'We don't normally get scooters stopping outside the guesthouse at that time of night. I heard the engine and decided I ought to check it out. I was sure it was you who dismounted from the back of it.' Véronique hid her smile in her orange juice.

Marion remembered how attentive François had been all that evening before thinking about the lack of response from Richard. Of course, she could sort all this out very quickly by asking Véronique about the phone call. But how stupid would that make her look? She did not want to air her dirty washing in front of Véronique, no matter how much she had come to like her.

Marion had decided quite early on that Véronique was the sort of person people could not help but confide in. She appeared to be genuinely interested in what they had to say and took the time everyday to talk. Guest and landlady boundaries did not exist. Véronique would offer to make a cup of tea when she thought you needed it or put out a plate of meat and cheese if, after listening to your day, she thought you might be hungry. People naturally gathered around her — a bit like a mother hen because they knew she would look after them. Marion was no exception.

'Would you like an aperitif? I know it's a bit early but Pascal and I opened a new bottle of Pineau rose this lunch time, it's nice and chilled, the perfect drink in this heat.'

Marion nodded. It was as if Véronique understood exactly how she was feeling at that moment.

The Pineau was sweet, yet cut like a knife as it slid down. Marion felt instantly light headed.

'He's full of charm isn't he?' Véronique said, continuing in the same vain.

Marion smiled remembering the beguiling way François had greeted her at the harbour. 'He's French, doesn't it come with the territory?' she replied.

'Pascal would certainly agree with that,' Véronique said, laughing. 'You can tell me to mind my own business,' she continued, 'but just how did you get to be on the back of his scooter?'

'He wrote me a note asking me out for the evening and I foolishly said yes.'

'Did he tell you about Natalie?'

'He told me that he used to be married but that was all.'

'I only mentioned it because he has shied away from women since. He must consider you different.'

'Maybe he just wants company,' Marion said, knowing what that felt like. 'The problem is I don't want to give him the wrong idea. We had a lovely time but my life is complicated enough.'

'Have you spoken to him today?'

'No, he was expecting me to go to the bar but I thought it best to stay away.'

'I'll let you into a little secret,' Véronique said. 'French men like to know where they stand. None of this saying you'll contact them and then not doing so nonsense. He will expect you to be honest with him and tell him if you don't want to see him again, and something else, everything you hear about French men being passionate and intense is true. If he's asked you out, he's serious.'

Marion imagined there must be plenty of women who would give their right arm for a passionate French man to be a part of their lives. However, at this moment in time, *she* was not one of them. It would mean she had given up on her marriage, on something she still believed in. She could not dismiss eighteen years of her life where, for the most part, she had been happy, to let herself be swept into some schoolgirl holiday romance. She would have only eight days with François then she would have to leave and go back to the real world. There was no point in making it more difficult for herself.

The Pineau had gone straight to her head. She knew it was a mistake to drink alcohol; the heat had dehydrated her, and she had only eaten a small ham baguette at lunchtime. She politely finished the last of the pink liquid before excusing herself. She went up to her room to lie down. With the combination of the heat and the alcohol, she wanted nothing more than to close her eyes.

When she woke some hours later, the light had begun to fade. She felt groggy and a little nauseous without having eaten anything for a while. The thought of a three-course meal in a restaurant turned her stomach even more. She would ask Véronique to make her some toast; it was all she wanted.

After splashing her face with cold water and brushing out her hair that curled in waves around the contours of her cheekbones, she made her way tentatively down the stairs to the kitchen, feeling a little faint but trying to ignore it. Without warning, she swayed and the floor hurtled towards her.

'*Oh mince!*'

She recognised the voice. Strong arms folded around her and gently lowered her on to a chair.

'Marion, look at me!'

She lifted her head and stared straight into the concerned eyes of François.

'Here give her this,' Véronique said, soothingly.

François took the glass of water from her and placed it in Marion's hand. 'Drink,' he said more insistently.

'*Oh La La!*' a voice behind caused them all to turn and look. Pascal had entered the scene from the dining room where he had been finishing off his Camembert and red wine.

Veronique shooed him away with a flick of her hand. There was no room for any more bystanders; Marion needed air not suffocating.

Marion took small sips of water, emptied the rest of the glass and began to feel better. She looked around, two pairs of anxious eyes belonging to François and Véronique darted over her face.

'Are you all right?' François spoke first. 'When was the last time you ate anything?'

Marion had to think hard, her head was still groggy. 'I had a sandwich for lunch.'

'Is that all?' he said, horrified. 'You're not in England now. Here we eat properly. A hearty plate of food, none of these snack meals, that way you are less likely to faint with hunger,' he chided.

She twisted the empty glass in her hand. He was scolding her like a naughty child.

François looked at his watch. 'You haven't eaten in eight hours.'

He sounded appalled. He was being so authoritative about it all. Marion omitted to tell him about the ice cream in case she got another lecture.

'Right! No arguments. I'm taking you out.'

'But it's late!' She resisted.

'Late for what? You English go out at six o'clock and are tucked up in bed by nine. In France at that time, we are only just getting started.'

He turned to Véronique, 'I'll take her to Pierre's.'

Marion did not care where they went. François was looking after her; she could not remember the last time Richard had done that.

'I need to get dressed,' she said, looking down at the shorts she had been wearing all day.

'It doesn't matter what you're wearing. Although some shoes would be useful,' he said, smiling.

Véronique ran upstairs to Marion's room and returned with her sandals and a cardigan.

At the restaurant, Pierre came out of the kitchen to greet them. He was of similar build to François but Marion suspected his girth was more to do with food than any muscle. There followed a flurry of French, accompanied by a vigorous handshake, a slap on the shoulder and peals of laughter. It was obvious to her that they knew each other well. In contrast, he politely shook Marion's hand. His eyes never left her face. What is it, she thought, with these French men and their intense stares.

The restaurant was small and quaint with dark wooden furniture, soft lighting and green tablecloths.

She sat at a table whilst the two men disappeared into the kitchen. A young waitress came to light a small candle housed in a glass jar in the middle of the table. *'Bonsoir ,'* she said, gaily.

The aroma of tomato, cheese, and garlic hung in the air, all the while teasing Marion's taste buds. She needed to eat and began to peruse the menu unsure how much she could really manage. Although she felt heaps better, her stomach was doing tiny somersaults. She had not expected to be out for a second time with François.

'You won't find what you're going to eat on there.' He returned smiling, apparently keen to remain in charge of the situation. 'I explained to Pierre what happened earlier. He's going to prepare you one of his special pasta dishes. You need energy.'

He moved his chair from the opposite side of the table bringing it round next to her.

'I'm not going to faint again.' She laughed. 'There's no need to get ready to catch me.'

The proximity of his body made her nervous. His cologne was intoxicating, his face, close to hers. If she leant forward slightly she could kiss him. He was looking at her in earnest.

'I think we should talk,' he said.

She watched the waiter bring him a glass of beer. If she was going to have to bare her soul, or the very least explain about Richard, she would have preferred some alcohol herself. Instead, she settled on water as the sensible option.

Opening up to him made her feel vulnerable. He was already chipping away at her defences; she needed to maintain control. Any serious conversation with him scared her.

'What do you think we should talk about? The weather, or the price of fish,' she said trying to remain calm.

François took a sip of his beer. 'I don't know about the price of fish,' he said, flatly.

She smiled, 'I was only joking.'

'You don't want to tell me why a beautiful woman has come on holiday on her own, and why, after spending a very pleasant evening together, you avoided me today.'

She fidgeted; uncomfortable with the conversation, knowing he was not going to give up and that he deserved an explanation.

'I just needed to get away for a while,' she said finally, and told him about Richard's attempts to stop her.

François shook his head in disbelief. When Marion recounted her escape in the middle of the night, he laughed aloud. 'You are one determined lady. You have courage and strength, I admire that,' he said softly, his eyes full of affection.

'Well I was determined Richard wasn't going to stop me coming here if that's what you mean.'

'Did I offend you in any way last night when you agreed to meet me? Maybe I was too presumptuous. You are an attractive woman Marion. I couldn't treat you as if you don't exist. Your husband is a fool.'

Their food arrived at that precise moment. Marion was glad for the interval; her head was spinning and not just because she had not eaten for a while. Her pasta came in a small dish with chunks of cooked fresh salmon stirred into a crème, tomato and basil sauce. It was delicious. She ate hungrily, reprimanded by François to take it steady or she would end up with indigestion. At his request, Pierre had made a special seafood pizza for him, heavy on the garlic and squid.

They ate in silence but every time Marion glanced at François, he was staring at her. She was more comfortable with it now and no longer wished he would stop; it made her feel special. Out of the corner of her eye, she glimpsed her handbag on the floor and half expected the beep of a text from Richard to intrude ironically on the moment.

After a while, intense fatigue overcame her. She had spent a long time walking that day in the heat. She intended to ask about Natalie — François' ex wife, but at that moment she stifled a yawn, not enough that François did not see.

'It's time I took you back.' He stood up and pulled the chair out for her. He placed his hand lightly on the small of her back as if taking possession just as he had done yesterday evening, and guided her to the door.

'*Excuse moi. Un moment,*' he said and left her whilst he popped his head into the kitchen to say goodbye to Pierre.

Outside the restaurant, a thousand twinkling stars littered the night sky. They resembled the eyes of lost souls observing them from on high. The same spirits that had born witness to her escape from Richard nearly a week ago, now watched her without hesitation, slip her arms around the firm waist of François on the back of the scooter. The tiredness swirled around her head like a fog. Her eyes grew heavier. She wanted to rest her head on him and fall asleep.

At the guesthouse, instead of kissing her hand he lent forward and brushed her cheek with his lips. 'Have you ever been sailing?' he asked.

Warily she replied. 'No. Why?'

'A friend has a boat moored in the harbour; we could take it out on my day off.'

She smiled. 'Another first.'

His brow furrowed.

She laughed at his bemused expression. 'I rode a scooter for the first time with you and now you're taking me sailing — for the first time.'

'I am happy to be making such an impression on you,' he said, truthfully.

'*À demain?*' He waited expectantly for her to reply.

Her voice came out in a whisper. '*À demain.*'

She turned and walked into the guesthouse. It was no use fighting how she felt. She wanted to see him again.

18

The shrill ringing sound woke Marion. The room was in darkness except for a slither of light that penetrated the tiny gap beneath the closed shutters. It was not enough to offer any illumination. She had no idea what time it was and could not remember setting an alarm. Eventually she realised it was her mobile phone making the noise. Still drugged with sleep, she answered it without thinking.

A familiar voice on the other end of the phone jolted her to her senses. She switched on the bedside lamp; it cast a soft orange glow across the corner of the room. She sat up and with her spare hand pulled at the pillows behind her before sinking back into them. Her head felt groggy from being woken so abruptly, and she cursed her own carelessness.

Richard was pleading in her ear. 'Marion please listen to me. I've been really stupid. I panicked, yes I made up the phone call, but only because I didn't want you to go. You'd obviously made up your mind; it was all I could think of to stop you.'

At last, the truth she had been waiting for, expecting even, but not relishing hearing. Now, she was wide-awake. She tugged at the pillows and sat upright.

'And the e mail to Véronique? How embarrassing do you think that was for me? She must have thought she was getting a mad woman as a guest for a fortnight.'

'Who's Véronique?'

'The owner of the *Chambres d'hôtes*. Thankfully, she hasn't mentioned the matter since.'

'I'm sorry about that too,' he whimpered.

There it was again that empty word. So easy to say but in Richard's case, so difficult to mean.

'You do understand why I'm here?' Marion asked him, her head still reeling from his revelations. 'Why I had to get away. If you had genuinely not wanted me to come, there was an easier way to prevent all this. Why must you always pick a fight with me?'

François had told her he could never treat her like that.

'Look, we can't sort this out over the phone. Come home Marion, I miss you.'

Marion was angry with herself for answering the phone and resented Richard for waking her up.

'Miss me for what exactly? Cooking for you? In fact generally looking after you.'

'Of course not!' He faltered, 'I can make a mean bolognaise sauce now with red wine.'

For a moment, Marion softened, and imagined him smiling. It evoked memories of when they first met, how he had impressed her with his culinary skills. She had always teased him about those days, saying she only married him because he could cook. Annoyingly, after the wedding, he had never cooked another thing. He left it all to her.

'Well at least something good has come out of this, but I'm not coming back till the end of the holiday,' she announced firmly.

'I love you Marion. I can't lose you.'

Marion sighed with frustration. Why did he have to pick now to say what she had wanted to hear for months?

'We'll talk about it when I get home.'

She quickly pressed *call end* before he could say anything else.

The first faint rumblings of thunder began as she went down for breakfast. By the time she had finished eating, the storm was attacking with vengeance. Each clap was in surround sound and impossible to ignore. She watched as the rain lashed at the windows and the flashes of lightening danced from one part of the sky to another, trapping her in the guesthouse.

'Oh this is normal!' Véronique told her. 'The temperature climbs little by little over a period of time, then bang! Along comes a storm cooling everything down and the whole process begins again. Pascal will be relieved; he hates the heat and it will save him having to water everything in the garden morning and night.'

After breakfast, she went back to her room and tried to read her book but she found it difficult to concentrate. The disturbance outside was nothing compared to the turbulent emotions that were churning around inside her. Backed into a corner, Richard had finally admitted what she had always suspected. However, it did not make her feel any better knowing she had been right. If anything, she felt more despondent. An element of mistrust had now crept into her marriage. How would she know that Richard was not lying to her again when it suited him to do so?

By lunchtime, the storm had moved away, but the rain stayed.

'Intermittent heavy showers for the rest of the day,' Véronique told her when she ventured downstairs.

'Do you have an umbrella I could borrow?' Marion asked her.

Véronique smiled and handed her a black one with the Eiffel tower randomly printed in grey over the surface of the material. 'You must be eager to go somewhere if you're willing to get wet.'

'I am actually. I need to thank François for last night.'

Véronique gave her a knowing look and smiled. Even Pascal had commented on how Marion's eyes shone. She had lost that fretful look; instead, her face was more relaxed, smiling. It had not gone unnoticed that her hair, normally worn tied back, was now brushed loose. It flowed in thick auburn waves over her shoulders. She wore the slightest hint of make-up, a little mascara and a pale lip-gloss and her cheeks had a rosy bloom from the sun.

'Be careful,' Véronique said.

Marion smiled knowing what she meant.

Outside, the heavy rain had disturbed the dry soil; the air smelt earthy and was much cooler and fresher. A pale grey blanket of clouds replaced the earlier dark, stormier ones.

Marion zipped up her waterproof jacket and walked briskly, dodging the puddles. She made it to the bar before the next shower and sat in the covered section normally reserved for diners. It was like sitting in a dead end tunnel. Dark grey canvas walls surrounded the tables on three sides, the front wall, facing the harbour had windows so as not to impede the view. She was the only person there and felt conspicuous.

François came out as soon as he saw her and bent to kiss her cheek. His eyes lingered on her face, smiling.

She blushed and lowered her eyes.

He laughed. 'How are you feeling today? I see you've heeded my advice and come to eat a decent lunch, not just a sandwich this time.'

She smiled and picked up the white menu card. 'So tell me, since you work here, what would you recommend?'

'*Le plat du jour.*'

'The what?'

'The dish of the day. It's grilled sardines with potatoes from the oven.'

A couple arrived having also braved the inclement weather for a bite to eat. François shook the man's hand then kissed the woman lightly on the cheek. Marion resumed reading the menu and left them to their lighthearted conversation. François, she thought, must know everyone. Even the holidaymakers became his friends. Was she not the perfect example? Just how many of them had he felt it his duty to save from some personal crisis going on in their lives? Was the time spent with her all part of the job, to keep the tourists happy, encouraging them to return for another holiday. If it was, he should have a post in the Government; he must be doing wonders for the French economy.

The couple sat down; François turned his attention back to Marion. 'Have you decided?'

'Yes. I'll have the dish of ...'

'*Le plat du jour*,' he corrected her, smiling. 'Did you know your name derives from the French name of Marie? I would like to teach you to speak a little of my language if you'll let me.'

His smile turned Marion's heart.

The young girl who had served her the other day brought her a carafe of water. She exchanged '*Bonjour*.' Marion was left alone to wait for her food.

In the bay, the tide was out. The sand looked more like mud in the grey light. A strong breeze continued to ruffle the pointed leaves of the palm plants, and coats replaced yesterday's shorts and t-shirts.

Gradually a few more hungry, wet souls, seated themselves in the bar. François was kept busy. From a distance, she watched him with the customers. Sometimes he appeared to be serious, polite, earning him respect and probably some good tips later. At other times, he was the François for whom she had become to feel great affection. He laughed, joked, chatted, and of course, there was always that cheeky smile, she had fallen for on her first day. No matter how hard she tried to fight them, like a drawbridge, her defences were being lowered slowly.

François arrived with her sardines and to her surprise sat back down opposite her. 'Tomorrow I will spend the day with Jean-Paul. Natalie is bringing him to see his grandparents.'

She realised she still knew nothing of his marriage. 'Do you see him often?'

'Whenever I get time off I go to Bordeaux, or I see him when he visits with Natalie. It's not often enough. I wanted him to live with me but Natalie has a job that pays more than mine does. She can offer him more.'

Marion saw the pain briefly in his eyes. Instinctively, she wanted to place the palm of her hand against his cheek, in a sort of friendly gesture of sympathy at his situation. She resisted the temptation.

François excused himself and left her to eat her meal. The sardines were delicious but a little tricky to eat being so small. When she had finished, it looked as if there were more parts of the fish left than the bit she had eaten.

The girl came to clear away her plate. She could see François charging around between tables. Without warning, he appeared and placed a *crêpe* in front of her, smothered in chocolate sauce.

'For Madame, who likes chocolate, a present from me.'

'Thank you.' She smiled. 'And thank you also for last night.' She lowered her eyes towards the *crêpe*. 'I haven't felt so cared for in a long time.'

Richard may have repented, but in her opinion, he had a long way to go to match François.

'Sunday we will go sailing,' he said. 'The weather is good. I will bring a picnic. Meet me over there at ten.' He pointed to the start of the concrete jetty. 'I have to go. *À dimanche*,' he said, softly.

'*À dimanche*,' she repeated.

19

Richard was disappointed that Marion had abruptly ended their telephone conversation. He had hoped to persuade her to cut short her holiday now that she seemed to have accepted his apology. It would have been even more agreeable if she had invited him to join her, turned the holiday into a romantic break for the two of them. Maybe, if he could find out exactly where she was staying in France, he could turn up unannounced and surprise her. His hopes soared at the thought.

He reached into the fridge for a beer, flicked off the bottle top and fetched Marion's laptop from the living room. He waited for it to spring into life before confidently typing in her mother's maiden name; the password she used for everything.

The computer rejected it.

He tried again in capitals. It rejected it for a second time. He was sure it was the one he had used previously. Frustrated, he tried other combinations, all failed to gain him access.

'Damn it!' he cursed under his breath. Marion had changed her password. He could not ask her for the name of the place she was staying because the idea was to surprise her.

He took a swig of beer and thought for a moment. She must have told Jodie where she was staying. He knew she would not tell him; she was Marion's best friend.

The first day of Marion's disappearance, he had badgered Carol to tell him where she had gone. Carol had acted as if she had no idea other than France. He sensed at the time she was being cagey; he wished he had been more insistent. He was well aware the relationship between the two sisters was strained. Carol did not like Marion interfering, she felt her sister had become too close to Alice, acting as if she were her own daughter. Although he had pointed this out to Marion on numerous occasions, and had tried not to take sides, he now saw how this rift could work in his favour.

Richard flinched as he took a sip of the pale brown liquid Carol had just handed him; it was bland, almost tasteless instant Nescafe. Not the deep, rich, ground coffee he was used to drinking.

'Are you sure Marion didn't give you any more clues as to where she is in France?' He placed the mug away from him on the table.

'She did say, but it's no good asking me to remember these French names.'

'You don't want to tell me, do you?' Richard suggested. 'Has Marion sworn you to secrecy?'

'Actually she hasn't,' Carol said, indignantly. 'It's beyond me why she's gone on her own. You two won't sort out your problems whilst you're in different countries.'

'Exactly! That's why I need to know where she is, so I can go and knock some sense into her.'

Carol glared at him. 'So you think Marion is the problem do you? You blame her for everything. My sister is many things, some of which I don't like, but I know that she loves you. If she wants to be alone now there will be a good reason. It takes two to make a marriage and usually only one to break it. I don't think Marion is the one.'

Richard hastily backtracked, realising his mistake. He had underestimated the rift between her and Marion. He thought he would have no problem persuading Carol to give her sister up. However, they were siblings, blood being thicker and all that.

'I've had my wakeup call Carol; I won't let it get this far again. Please, I need your help.'

Carol's shoulders relaxed.

'What if you saw the place on a map would you recognise it then? Richard asked. 'The article in the magazine mentioned a place called Royan. It might be near there.'

'What article? What magazine?'

'The one Marion deliberately left open for me to find the morning she absconded.'

'Why would she do that if she didn't want you to know where she had gone?'

'I don't know. Never mind.' He was getting impatient. He fetched up Google maps on her computer. Slowly, he scrolled down the coastline eventually stopping at Bordeaux. 'Recognise anything?'

'No, I think it began with an 'L'. La something.'

He scrolled back to Royan, then further north.

'There!' Carol shouted, she put her finger on the screen over the name. 'I'm almost certain that's the place. La Palmyre.'

Richard knew exactly what he needed to do next. 'Thank you.' He gave her a quick peck on the cheek. 'Let's hope your right.'

He went to pour his untouched coffee down the sink. There was no need to stay any longer.

He arrived home to find a grey Peugeot parked outside the house. As he stepped out of his car, Jodie appeared at the side of him. His mind jumped to allsorts of conclusions as to why she was here, none of them pleasant. Reluctantly, he invited her in.

She stood in the kitchen playing nervously with her car keys.

Richard noticed. 'You're not here on a social visit, I take it.'

'I'll come straight to the point,' she said. 'Kevin saw you at the Cocked Hat pub, kissing a blonde woman in the car park. I want to know what's going on, Richard. Marion is my best friend. Are you having an affair?'

'You've got a nerve coming to my house and accusing me. Of course I'm not!'

It was the truth. He was not having an affair anymore.

'Then what did Kevin see?'

'I don't know what you're talking about.'

Jodie placed the car keys on the table, pulled out a chair and sat down.

Richard remained standing, his arms folded across his chest, his stomach tense, his heart pounding. He wanted to tell her to leave. If he did that, she would know he had something to hide.

'I remember a time,' Jodie said, 'when you put Marion on a pedestal. When did she fall off it, in your eyes?'

Richard stared at her. He felt as if he had been hit in the stomach. She was right, there was a time he would have done anything for Marion; now he had let her down, betrayed her trust. He realised he had not spoken to anyone about losing Anna, about the effect it had on his marriage. He wanted to talk. Where was the harm in unburdening his feelings to Jodie? She would understand. He sat down and dropped his head in his hands.

To Jodie's surprise, he burst into tears. She waited, without saying anything.

After a few seconds, he pressed his eyelids with his fingers to quell the tears and wiped his wet cheeks with the palm of his hand.

'Everything fell apart after Anna.' His voice was flat. He stared emptily out of the kitchen window.

'Marion thinks you blame her.' Jodie said, softly.

'I know. She's wrong. What was there to blame her for?'

'I don't mean about losing the baby. I mean about making the decision not to have another child.'

'She didn't even talk to me; imagine that. I wasn't even consulted, as if my feelings didn't matter.'

'Is this what it's all about, Marion making a decision without you? She was scared. Could you not see that?'

'I still thought she was wrong at the time. What happened totally consumed her, nothing about me mattered. I know how that sounds now, self centred and selfish.'

He let out a despondent sigh.

Jodie looked at the man her best friend still loved, despite all the heartache. She prayed she was wrong about the affair. She had to know.

'Do you still love Marion?'

'I never stopped. I remember when I first set eyes on her in Johnny's nightclub on NewYears Eve. You were there.'

'I remember.'

'She wore a simple black dress, her hair was long and curly… and those green eyes. I thought she was too good for me. I couldn't even summon up the courage to speak to her. I fell in love that night. It hit me with such force. I had to see her again. I went back to the club, the following week, in case she went there regularly, but she never turned up. The barman didn't know who she was. Do you know how I found her?'

He laughed and relaxed back in the chair, he was on familiar ground, reminiscing about the good times.

'I was sat in the car on the ring road, waiting for the lights to change. I turned to look at the car that pulled up at the side of me. It was Marion. She was singing and tapping the steering wheel; she saw me laughing at her, then the lights changed. I followed her to the hospital. I had no idea if she worked there or if she was ill. I waited until she had disappeared into the entrance, then I went in and asked the receptionist if she knew her.'

'That's Marion Fletcher. She starts today as a nurse on A&E. Can I give her a message?'

'I told the receptionist I would call back later, then I went to buy some flowers. I left them at the reception and wrote my phone number on the card. Marion called me the next day. You know the rest... God I've been so stupid. I know where she is in France, Carol told me.'

'So what are you going to do?'

'I'm going to surprise her and hope for the best.'

'I meant about the other woman.'

'Clare?'

Jodie had been clever. He would say that for her. She had made him relax, open up, then pounced unexpectedly. He threw her a scared look, he had just admitted to having an affair.

'It's over,' he said quickly. 'Are you going to tell Marion?'

Jodie lent forward over the table. 'Not unless you put me in a position where I have to. I think we both know what I mean by that.'

'What if Marion and I patch things up without her knowing about Clare? Surely it would be best to keep it from her.'

'You'll have to be the judge of that. I just want Marion to be happy again. But if she ever finds out I knew and didn't tell her...'

'If I decide to tell her, I promise I won't mention you or Kevin.'

Jodie left a few minutes later. Richard went straight to the cupboard in the dining room where they kept the bottles of spirits; he poured himself a whisky. He hoped Jodie would keep quiet. It was up to him now.

Thanks to Carol, he had the name of the place Marion had gone to in France, and thanks to Marion, he had the name of the woman who owned the guesthouse where she was staying. It did not take him long to find the *Chambres d'hotes* run by Véronique and Pascal Dubois, and to learn that they had a single room available. He sent a booking request, lying about his name, in case Véronique told Marion and spoiled his surprise.

The last time he had felt this excited, he had arranged to meet up with Clare for the first time, anticipating that they would be in bed together before the evening finished. His ego had the better of him then. It had been the first time a younger woman; any woman had shown an interest in him other than Marion. He thought a mistress came with the territory of being a company Director. He had been an arrogant fool.

It had been a week since Clare had thrown him out. On the one hand, he was relieved he had not seen or heard from her in that time; on the other, somewhat disheartened to think she had easily moved on from him; out with the old, literally in his case. There was no denying he had fun with her, something he had considered was sadly lacking in his life at the time, but she was not Marion. Now, he only wanted to concentrate on making things right in his marriage. Despite what they had been through, Marion and he were still together, of sorts. He felt confident that had to mean something.

After booking his flight, he bounded upstairs to pack before bringing the suitcase down to the kitchen ready for loading into the car in the morning. He could not wait to see the look on Marion's face when he appeared at the guesthouse. Furthermore, he was looking forward to some elaborate French cuisine and a good bottle of Bordeaux red.

Whilst his frozen pizza came to life in the oven, he grabbed a bottle of beer from the fridge and stood flicking his way through the pages of the Daily Express newspaper.

According to the exchange rate, he was not going to get many Euros to the pound. France was going to be an expensive trip. Still, if he came back with his marriage intact it would be worth the price.

Just as he was taking the pizza out of the oven, the doorbell rang. He cursed, he was not expecting anyone and he was starving. For a moment, he debated whether to pretend no one was in. It rang for a second time.

'Oh for Gods sake...'

The minute he saw Clare standing there, he regretted opening the door. She was wearing a cream mac, the belt was tied, not fastened normally. For a brief second he wondered if she was naked underneath. It would not be the first time she had turned up to meet him minus her clothes. He caught his breath.

'Hello Richard, can I come in?'

She was the last thing he was expecting. He felt a rush of adrenaline. He wanted to slam the door in her face. What an earth was she thinking turning up at his house? What if Marion had been here? He was aware his pizza was getting cold and had no desire to have an argument with her on the doorstep. Reluctantly, he stepped aside to let her in.

'What do you want?'

Clare untied the belt of her mac. He swallowed hard. She slid it off her shoulders and threw it over the back of the pine chair; underneath, she was neither naked nor dressed to seduce him. He breathed a sigh of relief. She wore a short skirt and a t-shirt, not the usual cleavage-revealing top he was used to seeing her wear; nevertheless, it still accentuated her full breasts. He forced himself to avert his eyes from her chest and to fight the feeling of desire she still aroused in him.

'A coffee would be nice,' she replied, politely.

Richard looked at his ready to eat pizza, his taste buds salivating; reluctantly, he put it back in the oven. He was in no mood to share it; he wanted her to stay as short a time as possible.

Clare sat down at the table. She said nothing whilst Richard busied himself with the coffee maker. He placed two small coffee cups on the table and sat down with her.

She looked over towards the suitcase. 'Going somewhere?'

'On holiday,' he said sheepishly. It was best not to say where or who with.

'To France by any chance, to be with your wife.'

Richard almost spat out his coffee. She was too perceptive for her own good.

'So, what if I am? I thought I'd made it clear it's over between us.'

'Yes well, there's just one problem with that.'

'Oh? And what might that be?'

Clare paused and breathed deeply. 'I'm bloody pregnant.'

Richard felt sick. He stood up and went over to look out of the window at nothing in particular; he just needed some time to think. In disbelief, he pushed his hands threw his hair.

'Well, say something,' she demanded.

He turned to face her. 'Are you sure? Have you done a test?' He noticed his voice had moved up an octave. He coughed.

'I bought a test the day you dumped me.'

'So it's definite then?'

She bit her lip and nodded.

'How did it happen? I mean you were supposed to be on the pill. You didn't forget to take it did you?'

'Do you really think I would stoop so low as to try and trap you?'

That was exactly what had occurred to him; she had got pregnant deliberately.

'You think I did this on purpose don't you? I'm not stupid, Richard; we weren't even together properly. I'm not going to lumber myself with a child. Being a single parent is not a career choice I would pick.'

'Alright. Calm down. Have you thought what you're going to do?'

'What *I'm* ... I'll tell you what thoughts *I've* had: to tell *you*, so that *we* can decide together what *we* are going to do. Don't go thinking this is solely my problem.'

It was an easy decision for him; if she ended the pregnancy and found somebody else, he would not have to tell Marion.

'You'll have to have an abortion.'

The tears slowly rolled down Clare's cheeks.

He raised his eyes upwards in frustration and went to get the box of tissues. It was over between them. He just wanted to go to France, to be with Marion. Now, he had a baby to think about.

He went to the cupboard, poured himself a double shot of whisky and downed it in one. His heart was racing. In the space of two minutes, Clare had succeeded in turning his world upside down, again.

He wished he had never met her.

'I think I need one of those,' she pleaded.

'You can't.'

He looked at her. She looked a mess. He was surprised he had not noticed before. Her skin was pale, her eyes rimmed with black mascara. He felt a pang of guilt and poured her a half measure.

'For medicinal purposes only you understand. It's meant to be good for shock and I think we're both suffering from that.'

She toyed with the glass. 'Suppose I don't want an abortion.'

'But we're not a couple Clare. We never were. I can't give you the security you need, and like you said, you're not going to choose to bring up a baby on your own. Besides, it would destroy Marion if she knew I was going to have a child with another woman.'

'Oh! And you can't upset Marion but you can kill your child,' she spat at him.

'Shut up! Just shut up! You don't know the half of it.' He poured another double shot of whisky. He had to tell her about Anna; it was relevant under the circumstances.

'What don't I know?'

'Marion…we lost a baby when she was six months pregnant. Marion had to give birth knowing our daughter was already dead. As you can see, we didn't have any children after that.'

He threw back his head and tipped the contents of the glass down his throat to drown out the memory.

'Oh Richard! Why didn't you tell me?'

She went over to where he was standing. 'Don't you see. I can give you that chance to be a father?'

He glared at her. How could she be so cold, so shallow about it all, even if she was right? The whisky dulled his head, he could not think straight. He caught sight of the suitcase. It was a reminder that half an hour ago he was all set to spend a week with his wife. Now what was the point in going, to try to build bridges he might have to tear down later?

'You never did tell her about us did you, despite your promises.'

He shook his head. Truthfully, he would prefer to keep it that way if he could.

'What are we going to do Richard?'

She looked so vulnerable. He saw the fear in her baby blue eyes, the ones that had coaxed him into wanting to get to know her intimately. Instinctively, he reached for her and held her.

'I don't know. At least allow me some time to think.'

They clung, each seeking reassurance from the other. She lifted her head. Without hesitation, he kissed her. There was a need in him to feel close to her, as if by doing so, it would make everything seem alright. He was well aware Clare loved him and would do anything for him, yet it had been nothing more than straightforward sex for him, a bit of fun. He had never told her he loved her and meant it.

She was all over him now, her hands tugging at his t-shirt. He broke away, removed the coffee cups, and pulled her down underneath him on the table, burying his head in her neck. He pulled up her skirt.

'Richard. Stop!'

He pulled away from her. 'I'm sorry it's just . . .'

'I know, but not like this. Can I stay the night? Please. I don't want to be alone.'

He carried her upstairs and laid her on the bed. She reached for him, drawing him down on top of her. It was then he realised how much he had really missed her.

The morning light seeped through the curtains, waking him.

Clare slept on.

He looked at the clock on the bedside table, 'Shit!' He was supposed to be at the airport in half an hour. In his mind, he tried to assemble the events of last night, starting with why Clare was in his bed. It was like getting drunk and waking up not remembering anything about it; gradually the memories pop back up to the surface accompanied by regret if you were unlucky, and he was.

He grabbed his clothes off the bedroom floor and fled to the bathroom.

'Just look at you!' He shouted at his reflection in the mirror. 'You're weak, pathetic, you can't keep your hands to yourself. What are you going to say to her now? Thanks for one last time but I still want you to have an abortion.'

What a bloody mess. He was going to be a father, except it was with the wrong woman. He threw the plastic cup with his toothbrush and toothpaste across the room. It clattered against the side of the bath.

Clare started hammering on the door. 'Richard let me in. I think I'm going to be sick.'

He raised his eyes to the heavens and yanked open the door.

She pushed passed him and threw up in the toilet.

He left her to it, went down to the kitchen and pushed his suitcase out of sight under the stairs before slamming shut the cupboard door.

20

Marion could not stop thinking about François. She awoke early on Sunday morning feeling as if she had barely slept. Today they were going sailing and would be confined together on a boat, just the two of them. Her stomach was in knots at the thought of it.

'I hated sailing,' Véronique told her at breakfast. 'François' father used to take us out when we were younger. I was always ill and cold, and wet.'

'Thank you for that reassurance,' Marion said.

On Véronique's advice, she had bought herself some suitable footwear — a pair of pumps from one of the shops in town, and wore navy blue shorts and a white t-shirt. She had rolled a waterproof up inside her bag, just in case.

As she headed for the harbour, a slight breeze fluttered the tips of the palm trees; the sky was a deep blue and the clouds wispy.

Yachts and windsurfers were already zigzagging about the bay. She spotted François loading a bag on to the boat, a *baguette* poked out from the top of it. She set off to join him, her feet treading hesitantly on the metal walkway.

François saw her approaching and waved. He was wearing the broadest of smiles. His white t-shirt showed off just how tanned and muscular he was.

She lifted her arm to wave back. When she reached the boat, he kissed her on both cheeks, hovering briefly over her lips in the process. Marion felt her heart skip. She accepted his outstretched hand and stepped aboard.

The boat swayed slightly as her feet landed. Instinctively, she grabbed hold of François to steady herself. She felt the taught muscles of his arm circulate her waist in response. He smiled. 'You'd better get used to that. We'll be doing a lot of swaying from side to side today.' His eyes, laughing, searched her face and once again came to rest on her lips.

'If you're trying to frighten me it's working,' she said. In an effort to put some distance between them, she pointed to the two wooden doors at the front of the boat. 'What's down there? Can I have a look?'

François released her, she moved forward gingerly, aware that with every step she took, the boat tilted slightly. Curious, she poked her head inside. There were two settee births, topped with blue and white striped material, on either side of a wooden table, screwed to the floor. Another, double birth, was moulded into the front of the boat. Marion found herself wondering if François brought other women sailing, and if so, did he make love to them on the bed?

He came to stand behind her, 'There's a toilet in there.'

She spotted the door he was referring to.

'You have to pump the water to flush, it's not complicated.'

They both moved backwards from the doors. François pointed over the top of the large stone boulders that made up the harbour wall. 'Out there,' he said, 'is freedom.' The emotion resonated in his voice. 'For me there really is nothing like it.'

She watched him stare out to sea as if immersed in another world. This was a part of François's life, she knew nothing about; in fact, she knew very little about him at all.

Richard did not have any hobbies. He did not seem to be driven by a passion to do anything. She suspected his motivation for going to the gym was purely vanity.

François reached into the cabin and fetched out a red life jacket. She stood obediently whilst he slipped it over her head and bent to secure the strap around her waist. The scent of his cologne lingered between them. His jaw line was darkened with stubble. She wanted to run her fingers over it, over his mouth, to touch his lips.

He raised his head. 'How does that feel?'

'Fine,' she replied quickly, embarrassed by her thoughts.

She stepped away from him and sat down whilst he started up the motor and swiftly untied the ropes that bound them to the jetty. As soon as they were out of the shelter of the harbour wall, Marion felt the wind on her face. Her skin tingled from the salt.

They followed the line of green and red buoys that guided them through the deeper waters of the bay, and kept them from being stuck on any sand banks. Once out in the open sea, François reduced the speed of the engine.

'Come here,' he said. She moved to sit next to him. He reached for her hand and placed it under his on the tiller. His fingers were strong and firm and curled around hers reassuringly.

'Keep the front of the boat pointing in the direction of the headland over there while I put up the sails.'

Marion did as she was told; treating it as a test she must not fail.

François unclipped the small foresail at the front of the boat; it flapped wildly. Then he pulled on the mainsail until it had reached the top of the mast and secured it in place. He set the sails and replaced Marion at the tiller, killing the engine, he told her to remain next to him to balance the boat.

They quickly picked up speed. The stronger gusts of wind caught in the sails causing the boat to tilt occasionally, Marion grabbed hold of the edge of the boat to steady herself.

'Are you alright?' François shouted, his words carried away by the wind.

Marion nodded. She was not entirely comfortable when the boat listed, she had to trust that François knew what he was doing and would keep her safe.

The boat followed the coastline of golden beaches. Sun worshippers and bathers dotted the sand and surf, and the remains of concrete war fortifications endured; a constant reminder to all of the past conflict.

After a few minutes, Marion caught him staring at her and not at the headland, as he had told her she had to do earlier. Before she could say anything, the foresail began to flap vigorously, the mainsail swayed from side to side.

'Keep your head down.' François shouted at her.

The boat rocked violently throwing Marion on to the deck. She screamed.

François pulled hard on the tiller, the boat turned and the sails puffed out as if a giant breath had been blown into them.

Marion pulled herself up on to the seat, dazed.

'Are you alright?' François urged.

Her eyes, wide with fear, told him she was not.

'Don't move,' he ordered.

She watched him start up the outboard motor. It gave out a deep gurgling sound as it churned up the seawater at the back of the boat. He released the foresail; it crumpled onto the deck, and pulled down the mainsail.

The boat drifted, controlled only by the engine.

He sat down close to her and saw her eyes glistening with tears.

She tried to laugh it off, but it has scared her. 'I thought I was going to go overboard.'

'I'm sorry, are you hurt? It was my fault; I was too busy looking at you.' He reached for her. His mouth, sort hers. His kiss was gentle.

She did not have the strength to resist and brought her arms up to encircle his neck. For a moment nothing else mattered, François was kissing her, caressing her hair. She thought of Richard and was flooded with guilt. She pulled away, dropping her arms.

François released her.

'I can't,' she gasped.

'Forgive me,' he pleaded. 'I hoped you felt the same.'

He looked to Marion like a little boy lost. 'I'm sorry. It's just that Richard sits at home waving an olive branch and I'm spending the day with you. I can't help it, deep down, it doesn't seem right somehow.'

He cupped her face in his hands. 'Richard can go on waving until his arm falls off. I don't care. You're beautiful Marion. I love you. When was the last time your husband said those things to you?'

She could not remember Richard saying anything to her with such passion as François had just done. Even in those early, heady days of first love. She lowered her eyes.

'No, I didn't think so. But maybe it was too soon.' He relented. 'I'm French; we do and say what we feel. We are not as reserved as your British men.'

Marion looked at him. She could not help having these guilty feelings because she had betrayed Richard. She loved him but for what… the sake of the good times? They seemed like a distant memory now. She thought back to the last conversation. Although he had been remorseful about everything, would she ever be able to feel for him what she was feeling for François right now?

He stroked her cheek. 'We can take this as slowly as you like,' he said.

She nestled her head into his shoulder and closed her eyes. His lips rested on her head, drinking in the smell of her hair. All the while, he made soothing, circular movements with his fingers on the back of her neck.

They motored into the small bay off St Palais. Marion recognised it instantly from their first evening together. The bar on the terrace, where they had begun to learn all about each other, was full of diners; a few people remained sunbathing on the beach, undeterred by the intense heat of the midday sun.

François dropped the anchor over the front. The boat drifted slowly one way then the other, its bow held fast by the anchor rope. He rigged up a temporary sun canopy.

Marion excused herself and went below to use the toilet. She managed the flush system and to wash her hands in the trickle of water from the tap to the wash hand basin.

Up on the deck, François had laid out a picnic. They feasted on *Fois Grois* and *Camembert*, washed down with a large glass of red wine.

After lunch, he stretched out on the seat and placed his cap over his face like a 'do not disturb' notice.

It was getting hotter.

The surface of the sea shimmered, enticing Marion into its cool depths. The wine made her feel reckless. She had never been skinny dipping before. It would be another first she could add to her list. The water was freezing. She was unable to draw breath for the first few seconds before gradually relaxing and embraced the feeling of freedom and sensuality that accompanied swimming naked.

The splash woke François. He jumped to his feet and rushed over to the side of the boat where he last saw Marion sitting, before he fell asleep. There was no sign of her. He shouted her name in earnest and made his way to the bow. After finding her clothes in a pile on the deck, he caught sight of her, swimming below him on her back, her head tilted to catch the sun. He caught a glimpse of her white breasts under the shallow water.

She brought her head upright and saw him watching her. Laughing, she flipped on to her front.

Now he could see the outline of her bottom.

'Don't look,' she shouted. I want to get out.'

François smiled. 'Not yet, I'm coming in.'

Uninhibited by Marion's presence, he swiftly removed his clothes and joined her.

They swam naked together. Playfully splashing each other like excited children. Whenever he made a move towards her, she swam away, laughing. When they had enough, François brazenly climbed up the back of the boat. He gathered up his clothes and went down into the cabin, allowing her to climb aboard unseen.

Once dressed, Marion made her way to the back of the boat. François was busy preparing to raise the mainsail. His wet hair glistened in the sun light. He smiled knowingly at her.

How much of her naked body had he seen, she wondered. She felt a strong desire to kiss him again and drew a sharp intake of breath, but shyness overcame her.

He moved away up to the front of the boat.

The moment was lost.

Together they raised the sails. The boat eased up and down on the waves; the breeze took them homewards.

Marion sat in the crook of his arm, the proximity of his body set her senses on fire. Every now and again, he pulled her closer towards him, she pretended to ignore it, but could not hide her smile.

'You never told me about Natalie?' she said.

'What is there to tell? She ran off with another man, richer and better looking than me,' he replied.

He turned the boat onto a close - haul, the sails held rigid against the wind and the boat picked up speed.

Marion held on tight to the edge of the boat to steady herself.

'Women don't run off with other men unless they are unhappy, and I can think of worse men to be with than an attractive barman,' she said timidly. 'There must be more to it.'

François turned the boat slightly, away from the direction of the wind this time, the sails became less taught and the boat slowed down.

'I wasn't always a barman. When I left school, I had an apprenticeship to be a mechanic. I fixed Natalie's car, that's how we met. Then the owner of the garage where I worked became ill. He spent eighteen months in hospital; they couldn't find out what was wrong with him, he had a blood disorder, I think. Anyway, his son took over in his absence. We had different opinions on how the business should be run and in the end he sacked me.'

They were approaching the entrance to the bay, the sun shone bright and low, the tide was on its way out slowly exposing the sandbanks beneath it.

'We'll have to lower the sails soon and motor the rest of the way,' François said.

'So, Natalie left you because you lost your job?'

'No. She left me because she didn't marry a barman who worked unsociable hours. The money wasn't as good either, even with the tips. She had an affair. When I found out, she left to be with him and took Jean-Claude with her. He will be seventeen soon, he can make up his own mind who he wants to be with, I hope he'll go to university and make something of himself, unlike his father.'

'I think your job is very important. When people come on holiday they want to find a nice bar with friendly staff, somewhere they can have a good time. Don't underestimate the part you play in that.'

'So, am I playing a big part in how much you are enjoying your holiday?'

She looked directly at him. 'More than you realise.'

He smiled.

They lowered the sails and motored in to the harbour. Marion took off her life jacket and placed it back inside the cabin. She glanced over to the bed. What so nearly could have been, she thought, had she not been so reticent.

They wondered up to the bar, windswept, tired, and thirsty. The girl, Marion now knew as Lisa, brought them a drink whilst they sat side by side staring out over the sea.

Marion made a mental note never to forget any part of today, she did not want it to end. It would always be etched on her mind and in her heart, as a constant reminder that life should not be empty and lonely as it had been. Whatever the future held for her, she would remember the happiness she had felt with François by her side.

They ate braised pork on a bed of Mediterranean vegetables with polenta, and shared a bottle of red wine whilst the sun set behind the lighthouse in the crook of the bay.

Marion wanted to remain there forever. There was nothing in her life in England that she could compare to this.

They took a short cut from behind the bar back to the guesthouse. François held her hand as they walked. Marion did not resist when he pulled her behind a tree and kissed her as she clung to the taut muscles in his back. She felt alive, buzzing with excitement. All the way home, she battled with the desire to suggest that they went back to his apartment. However, she had the feeling that François would not take her up on the offer, not tonight. He had made it clear on the boat that he cared too much for her to rush things. If she was going to be unfaithful to Richard, she did not want to have any regrets afterwards.

The following morning Marion was the last down to breakfast.

'Don't disappear, I want to hear all about it,' Véronique whispered to her as she placed the pot of tea and the basket of croissants and bread on the table. She almost shooed the remaining two couples out of the dining room. She returned with a cup of coffee and sat down opposite Marion. 'Well? How did it go? Were you sick? Did you hate it?'

Marion spread some raspberry jam onto her bread, deliberately taking her time just to tease her friend. She smiled, 'I loved it, apart from the bit where I fell on to the deck. But it was worth it in the end,' she gushed.

'So you enjoyed yourself with my cousin as well as the sailing?'

'Is it that obvious?' Marion laughed.

'Oh! Rosy cheeks, shiny eyes; of course it could just be from the wind and sun on the boat.' Véronique smirked.

'Do you think it's possible to love two men at the same time?' Marion asked her.

'Doesn't this happen the world round? I mean, men love their wives but will have a mistress. Women love their husbands but take lovers. Why? Because they can be flirtatious, it makes them feel alive; they are *in* love. With their partners it's a different kind of love, someone to set up home with, share the tedious responsibilities of life with, and of course satisfy the desire to have children.'

Marion shuffled uncomfortably and turned to stare out of the window.

'I've just said something I shouldn't have, haven't I?' 'I've upset you. I didn't mean …'

Marion picked up her napkin and played with the corner of it. 'I lost a baby when I was six months pregnant. There was no medical reason for it. It was an awful time. I didn't dare risk trying again for another, so we never had children.' She lay the napkin back on the table.

Véronique placed her hand on Marion's and gave it a squeeze. 'And your husband, how did he deal with it all?'

'He wanted us to have another. When I told him I couldn't bring myself to go through it all again, he… he changed. I saw less and less of him.'

'But you still love him?'

Marion nodded. 'I feel so guilty. If your theory is right, I love Richard but I'm *in* love with François. Although I suspect it might be more of a middle age cry for help.'

They both laughed.

'I have four days left before I have to face Richard and my old life. What would you do in my position?'

'When you came here, you were sad. Pascal was most concerned about you. He said you needed a French man to take you under his wing, make you smile again. He thinks all French men are born Lotharios.' She raised her eyes and smiled at Marion.' But it looks like he was right. You have blossomed. Happiness has replaced the sadness in your eyes, if it is only to be for a brief period, cherish it. As for feeling guilty, if you are referring to your decision not to have children, we all do things we regret and have to live with. It doesn't mean they have to shape the rest of our lives.'

Marion almost skipped down to the bar. When she arrived, there was no sign of François. She ordered a coffee and waited, giddy at the thought of him. Did she look like a middle-aged woman having just found excitement in her life? Because that is how she felt. Véronique was right; it was time to stop feeling guilty, it was in the past, and Richard could have found someone else younger than her to have children with if he was so desperate for them. She needed to consider *her* happiness. If it was to be with Richard, well that was fine, but if they could not make it work, she would just have to deal with it. One thing was certain; she was more ready than she had ever been to face the future.

21

Francois had requested the afternoon off work so that he could take her somewhere for lunch. Marion had decided it was the perfect occasion to try out Alice's cream sundress with the orange and yellow swirls; she twirled around in front of the mirror. It fitted perfectly.

'You look pretty today,' Francois commented. 'Not that you don't look pretty everyday, it must the dress. Is it new? You've never worn it before.'

She did not dare tell him she was wearing the dress of a seventeen year old.

'Where are we going?' she asked.

'To feast on oysters; you said you had never tasted them. Well, today will be another first for you.'

She smiled; there seemed to be a first time for everything with François.

La Tremblade was a small town on the right bank of the *La Seudre* estuary. The road leading down to the small fishing port ran alongside one of the inland canals that came off the estuary. It was low tide and numerous small sailing boats had become beached in the mud. On the opposite side of the road to the canal, a few restaurants were dotted in between a number of buildings that first appeared like old worn out shacks, but on closer inspection, they were places to buy and eat a selection of shellfish along with a glass of wine. The whole area resembled a fisherman's back yard. Behind the restaurants were the oyster beds — rectangular ponds of fresh water. In front, nets and wire cages, for catching crabs, lobster and crayfish were stacked high and dotted all around.

'I love it here,' François said. 'It has to be the most unpretentious place to bring you to try your first oyster.'

He parked the scooter in front of a long, single story, shed like building with floor to roof glass windows and a set of double doors at one end. Behind these, the shellfish were displayed as if on a market stall.

The choice overwhelmed Marion. She had no idea what half of them were.

François shook hands with the proprietor and ordered a platter of oysters and a plate of *grillon* — the local pâté, and a bottle of Sauvignon to accompany it all. Then he led Marion outside to a set of pale blue metal tables and chairs.

Once seated, he reached for her hand and kissed it.

'You look happy,' he said.

'I am. Is that wrong?'

'If something makes you happy, it can never be wrong,' he said.

She smiled at him, momentarily letting her hand linger in his.

The wine arrived; François poured them both a glass.

'What shall we make a toast to?' he said.

Marion thought for a moment, 'To happiness,' she replied. 'No matter how short,' and clinked his glass.

When the platter arrived, Marion eyed it nervously.

'Watch and learn,' François said mischievously.

Marion watched as he took an oyster shell and poured the contents into his mouth, chewed then swallowed.

She picked up a shell and did as François had just done. She grimaced. 'It tastes of salt.'

'It tastes of the sea,' he said. 'Have a piece of bread to cleanse your pallet then try another.'

The second one seemed not to have the same adverse effect; François did not observe any screwing up of her face.

'Well, what do you think now?'

'They're a taste to be acquired. I think I like them.'

'Good, you're becoming more French everyday.' He smiled at her. 'You know I've been in love with you ever since I first saw you. In French we call it *un coup de foudre.*'

Marion laughed. 'I think the oysters are affecting you, or the wine.'

'I'm serious, even trussed up in that life jacket you looked beautiful. The sun brought out the freckles on your nose. And as for that kiss...'

'Stop it,' she said, laughing. I've done enough blushing because of you.'

I know. French women have no problems accepting flattery, but you ... I like how vulnerable it makes you appear. It makes me want to take care of you for what little time we have left together.'

Marion swallowed hard, she was all too aware they would have to say goodbye in two days. She stared at him. His eyes were like whirlpools of dark chocolate in which she was drowning.

'Do you have to work this afternoon?'

'No. Not until this evening, why?'

She reached for his hand. 'I've never seen where you live.'

Marion did not remember anything about the journey to his apartment, she was only aware of the firmness of the muscles under his shirt as she held on to him on the back of the scooter. All the while, the closeness of his body against hers heightened her desire for him.

After opening the door to his apartment, he hesitated. She sensed he was waiting for confirmation from her that this was what she wanted. She slid her arms around his neck and he bent to kiss her, gently and slowly at first, then harder. He led her by the hand into the bedroom; she unbuttoned his shirt, passing her hands over the contours of his stomach then upwards seeking the softness of his dark chest hair. He sought her mouth, kissing her hard; swiftly and expertly, he undressed her, running his lips over every inch of her skin as he exposed it. Marion closed her eyes and let him transport her into a world of passion where François was in complete control, and where her imagination had taken her many times up to this moment.

After they had made love, François looked at her as if she was the most beautiful person he had ever seen.

22

Marion had passed the shop, with its racks of colourful dresses and tops displayed outside, many times, without stopping. This morning she bought a patterned green and orange sleeveless dress. François wanted to take her back to La Tremblade for their last evening together.

He was in the kitchen talking to Pascal when she went downstairs. He whistled when he saw her, passing his eyes slowly over the whole of her body.

She blushed.

François laughed aloud, so did Pascal. Marion saw the funny side and joined in.

Véronique entered from the dining room where she had been laying the last of the tables for breakfast. She took one look at Marion and turned to François, 'I hope you're not thinking of putting Marion on the back of a scooter in such a lovely dress.'

François looked embarrassed.

'Here.' Véronique handed him her car keys.

He threw her a grateful smile. 'Your carriage waits,' he said to Marion.

They went to a restaurant down by the port and sat outside on a covered wooden terrace next to the inland canal. The tide was in; the yachts and motor boats floated gently on their moorings. Above them, suspended lanterns gave out a soft, warm glow, and strands of twinkling fairy lights decorated the wooden beams. On each table, the flame of a small candle danced in the night air.

A bottle of Chardonnay, almost empty, sat in a silver ice bucket at the side of them, and discarded oyster shells lay on an oval platter in the centre of the table.

François looked every inch the stylish Frenchman in his white open necked shirt. He wore a thin gold chain around his neck; it was the first time Marion had seen it.

'Jean-Claude chose it for my birthday last year,' he told her, instinctively reaching up to touch it before entwining his hand in hers.

Mesmerised, she followed every move as he kissed each one of her fingers in turn, his touch soft and light caused desire to burn inside her. She took a sip of the crisp, white wine to cool her down.

He continued to play with her hand, rubbing with his thumb as if massaging her. 'I wish I didn't have to lose you from my life,' he said. 'Are you absolutely sure?'

'Sure about what?' Her voice sounded husky. She was so preoccupied with his touch she could barely speak.

'About going back to England, back to Richard,' he said.

Reluctantly she untangled her hand from his. 'We've had such a short time together, how will I know if this is just a middle age infatuation or if it's you I really love unless I go back?'

François murmured. 'For me it's simple, *Je t'aime,* stay with me, here, in France.'

Marion could not say that she loved him back because she truly did not know. Would she feel such desire, such excitement for him once she was back in England, back with Richard? The only thing she knew for sure was that this was the happiest she had felt in a long while.

'What if I stayed and I couldn't love you? Can't you see for both our sakes I have to do this? Please don't make it more difficult than it already is.'

'Alright, not another word.' He pretended to zip his lips.

She picked up the last oyster shell from the platter and tipped the creamy flesh into her mouth, savouring it for the final time.

'Can we go to the beach,' Marion asked him. 'The one I told you about, in the photograph. I want to see it before I leave.'

The tide was in; the waves fell gently, almost silently upon the sand. As they stood watching the last of the blood red sun sink into the ocean, Marion felt the tears well up inside her. After tonight, she knew she might not ever come here again.

She swallowed hard.

François placed his hand on the back of her neck and gently pulled her towards him. He kissed her eagerly before leading her by the hand back to the harbour.

Marion thought about tomorrow, having to leave François and face Richard. As if reading her thoughts François placed his arm around her, pulling her close, she rested her head on his shoulder. She had learned how to be happy again with François, how would she feel once she was home with Richard? The only thing she was certain about was how much she had changed. The woman that was returning home after two weeks in France knew exactly what she wanted if her marriage was to survive.

Back at his apartment, they made love. It was slow and sensual, along with the desire for each other was a need, a longing for it never to end.

Afterwards, François propped himself up on one elbow and stared at her intently.

'Promise me something,' he said. 'If ever you feel the need to escape again, you'll come here, to me.'

She reached up and touched his face. 'I promise.' She kissed him softly.

When it was time, it took all her inner strength to leave his side.

François watched as she picked up her discarded clothes from the floor and dressed. He insisted on walking her back to the guesthouse; she begged him not to. She could not face an emotional farewell in the middle of the street.

The tears trickled down her face as she closed the door to his apartment. On the horizon, the first streaks of daylight were beginning to form.

The tomorrow she had been dreading had arrived.

23

As the airhostess rambled on about emergency exits and oxygen masks, Marion watched in a daze. The man next to her carried on reading, immersed in his book, paying no attention to the safety demonstration being enacted in front of him. When the hostess got to the part about life jackets Marion smiled. She had a vivid memory of the last time she had been expected to wear one.

The plane rose into the sky leaving France behind and with it François. She missed his Jean Paul Gautier aftershave that lingered on her skin long after he was gone, his warm-hearted smile and his touch that left her tingling with excitement. It was hard to imagine she may never see him again. She turned to look at the disappearing land way beneath them. '*Au revoir*' my handsome Frenchman, her throat ached from holding back the tears.

The fresher air of England greeted her as she made her way down the aeroplane steps and into the terminal building. She joined the queue of melancholy holidaymakers returning home and snaked her way through passport control to the baggage reclamation. In the arrivals hall, loved ones hugged and kissed, nobody was there to meet her.

She was in no hurry to face Richard and took her time driving, hoping he had been called out to work; leaving her more time to prepare for what ever lay ahead. When she saw his BMW in the drive, she wanted to turn around and head straight back to the harbour, the beach, the bar, to laugh with Véronique and hug Pascal.

Richard heard the car pull into the drive. He went out to open the door for her, holding out his arms. 'I'm sorry, please let's not fight any more.'

Marion hesitated before climbing out of the car. When he hugged her, she experienced no fluttering of excitement or relief, no crashing of symbols or trumpet fanfares. She felt numb. *Give it time, this is what you wanted, a loving husband.* She lifted her head and placed a peck on his cheek.

'Shall I make a cup of tea? You must be in need of one.'

When was the last time Richard had offered to make her a cup of tea?

'I'll just go and change.' She needed space; it was all too claustrophobic.

Richard fetched the suitcase from the car and carried it upstairs.

The one person Marion had been excited to see was nowhere in sight. 'Where's Mimi?'

'She comes and goes to please herself,' Richard said. 'She'll be back when she's hungry.'

Marion began to unpack the case. Richard hovered as if he was a spare part in it all. She unfolded the dress she had bought in La Palmyre.

'That's nice,' Richard commented. 'Is it new? I haven't seen you wear anything like that before.'

She carried it over to the wardrobe and arranged it carefully on a hanger.

'I'll tell you what. Why don't you wear it tonight, we could go out to celebrate your return.'

She closed the wardrobe door. 'Another night. I'd like to stay in and have a bath, get used to being home again.'

'Shall I bring you a glass of wine?'

'No, I think I'll have a glass of this. She lifted a bottle out of the suitcase.

'What's that?'

'It's called Pineau, a fortified wine, like sherry, the French drink as an aperitif.'

'It sounds disgusting.'

'Well, I like it.'

'I'll fetch you a glass, then.'

She went into the bathroom and started to run the taps. Richard returned with the glass. Marion unscrewed the top of the bottle and poured herself a generous measure.

'Do you want a taste?' She held the glass out to him.

'No thanks. I'll stick to my beer.'

She carried the Pineau into the bathroom and closed the door behind her. On a shelf, at the side of the bath, were various candleholders. She took a match from the box kept there for the purpose and began lighting the candles. As she reached one of the holders, a wooden boat painted white, she stopped and ran her fingers over it, remembering the day she went sailing. When all the candles were lit, she took a sip of Pineau, it was just as she remembered it, the day she shared a glass with Véronique, the day François caught her in his arms as she fainted.

When the bath was ready for her to get in, she lay down in the warm water, it was not normal for her to feel this melancholy after a holiday; usually, when she and Richard went away she was happy to come home. But this had been no ordinary holiday. She had experienced for the first time what it felt like to go sailing, to eat oysters, to ride on the back of a scooter and to have a lover. Closing her eyes, she let the memories flood her thoughts.

Richard opened the bathroom door, quite sharply, bringing her back to the present. He poked his head around it, 'I wondered how long you would be? I missed you.'

She new what it was like to miss someone and responded with an empathetic smile.

'Don't be too long will you?' He closed the door.

Marion topped up the bath water; she wanted to stay with her memories for a while longer.

In the morning, Richard brought her breakfast in bed. Scrambled egg on wholemeal toast and tea. 'Sorry, it's not croissants.'

She pictured Véronique bustling around the dining room at the *Chambres d'hôtes*, serving up warm croissants with fresh, crusty French bread, and the lovely aroma of ground coffee that always greeted her. She was already missing her new friend; maybe she would send her an e-mail later and ask about François. Then again, she knew exactly how he would be feeling.

Out of the bedroom window, bathed in sunlight, the housing estates of Huddersfield stretched into the distance, topped by a solid mass of blue sky occasionally punctured by a wispy cloud. It was the sort of weather, her mum referred to as short sleeve weather. She wondered what her mum would have made of all of this, horrified, probably. She thought the sun shone out of Richard. She would not have dared tell her mum about François, in fact she would not tell anyone, including Jodie. Getting her marriage back on track was the important thing now and for that, her holiday romance had to remain a secret.

Richard cooked roast chicken for lunch with roast potatoes, carrots and green beans, and even helped her load the dishwasher.

In the afternoon, they went to the nearby Country Park and walked around the lake, stopping to watch the small sailing dinghies snaking their way across the water.

Sometimes the breeze would catch them suddenly, and the boat would tip on to one edge then roll back again as its owner steered it out of the wind. Marion smiled inwardly and became lost in her thoughts. The whole scene evoked a cherished memory of one of the happiest days of her life. She had made a promise to herself to recall that day if it all became too much for her again. It would be a reminder that she was not prepared to settle for anything less than being happy.

Richard told her he had to leave earlier than usual for work the following morning.

'I have to prepare for a meeting, I should have done it over the weekend, but I wanted to give you my full attention instead.'

Marion smiled coyly. 'You certainly did that. I can't remember the last time you put me before work.'

He kissed her goodbye on the lips. He could not tell her the truth. He had been summoned last night, by a text from Clare.

When she had imparted her news of the pregnancy, he had made her promise not to do anything rash, and to allow him to deal with Marion's return from France before he contacted her. He had spent the whole week in turmoil. Whichever way he looked at it, he would have to give something up.

He reversed out of the drive and drove straight to her house. Clare lived in a cul-de-sac. All the houses were small, almost built on top of each other, and the neighbours knew everyone's business. They would have been used to seeing his car parked outside in the evenings and knew he never stayed the night. He wondered what they made of him turning up at 7.30 in the morning.

They stood in her kitchen this time, a tiny box not big enough to swing a cat.

'Well, what have you decided?' she said.

'I don't know. It's not easy,' he shouted in frustration.

'Oh I think it is! Either you leave Marion or I'll have an abortion.'

An abortion, he knew, would solve everything. He could walk away from Clare and Marion need never know about any of it, yet it would be like playing God with someone else's life. Would he feel as if he was party to murder?

'How far gone are you?' he asked.

'Nearly two months.'

The longer he waited before making a decision… this was his last chance to be a father.

He still needed more time.

In his lunch hour, he went out and bought Marion a bouquet of cream roses and purple delphiniums. Purple had always been her favourite colour. He put some water in a bucket he found in the cleaners storeroom and placed them in the corner of the office.

His secretary eyed them jealously. 'Lucky woman,' she commented. She was dying to ask if they were to please the mistress or placate the wife but she was in no position to be able to afford to lose her job. Her mother had just been taken into a care home; she had to find the money each month to help pay for her.

'You're spoiling me.' Marion smiled when Richard arrived home and gave her the flowers. She kissed him before taking a glass vase from the cupboard. Painted on both sides with a single yellow rose, it was her favourite vase. After half filling it with water and arranging the flowers, she carried them into the living room and placed the vase on a small table.

Richard went upstairs to change, throwing his mobile phone on the bed, which simultaneously beeped with a text from Clare. He had told her never to contact him at home. The more she pestered him…

The aromatic smell of ginger and lemon grass drifted into the bedroom. He ignored the text, went down to the kitchen and found Marion cooking a Thai chicken curry.

She handed him a glass of wine. 'I never thought I would be saying this,' she raised her glass, 'here's to new beginnings.'

He clinked her glass but said nothing.

As she tossed the chicken and vegetables in the wok, he stood by and sipped his wine. He imagined Clare preparing a meal for him whilst he sat on the floor playing with their son or daughter. He had never tasted her cooking; they were too busy doing other things. It had been easier to order a takeaway. What if she complained about being too tired, what if he ended up having to do a day's work then have to cook and amuse the child at the same time. Would she look after him the way Marion was doing now?

He twisted his fork in the noodles absent-mindedly.

'What's wrong? Don't you like it?'

'What! No, it's not that, it's delicious.'

'Is there something you want to tell me?'

She remembered François's opinion that Englishmen always held back; they found it hard to be open with their feelings, unlike Frenchmen…

Richard shook his head and carried on eating.

'Because now, more than ever, we need to be honest with each other,' she said.

She was such a hypocrite; she was not being honest with him. There are something's worth telling and something's best kept hidden she had decided. Knowing about François would hinder, not help their reconciliation.

The phone rang in the hall. Richard's heart skipped a beat, surely, Clare would not… He immediately rushed to answer it, returning, he held the receiver out towards Marion. 'It's Carol for you.'

She took the phone from him.

'Oh Marion! Thank goodness you're there.'

'Carol! What's wrong?'
'I'm at the hospital. It's Alice; she's taken an overdose.'

24

Richard broke every speed limit there was on the way to the hospital.

'Thank God you only drank two glasses of wine,' Marion remarked. She twisted her hands on her lap. 'Why didn't she listen to me? I knew I was right.'

'Who?'

'Carol.'

'There was something really bothering her.'

'What are you talking about?'

'Alice, Of course!'

'You can't interfere, Marion. You're not Alice's mother.'

'I'm her Godmother. My job is to look after her.'

'When Carol is no longer around. She was very much alive the last time I saw her. Just tread carefully where her and Mark are concerned, especially Mark.'

Richard came to an abrupt halt in front of the entrance to A&E. Marion got out leaving him to go in search of a parking space. She trod the footsteps she made every working day in to the treatment area and cubicles. Sister Harding was on duty. She saw Marion hurriedly approaching, and ushered her in to the glass bowl of an office at the entrance to the ward. 'Before you go to pieces, Alice is going to be fine.'

Marion was not used to being on this side. She had trained to be standing where Sister Harding was now, comforting worried relatives. It felt strange to be one of them. Her face was full of concern as she stared bewildered at the Sister. 'What happened? Carol didn't make any sense on the phone.'

'Your sister said she found her behind the bathroom door, slumped on the floor. There were empty foils of Paracetamol beside her. We don't know how many she took. She was unconscious when they brought her in.'

'Have you pumped her stomach? Sorry! Of course you have.'

'Your sister's with her now. If you need to talk . . .'

Marion was already on her way out of the office.

Alice lay still with her eyes closed, as if she had been slipped inside the bed sheets like a doll into a pocket. Wires and tubes connected her to monitors and a drip, her long honeycombed hair splayed out on the pillow behind her, her skin sallow. She looked dead to Marion, like she had been laid out for viewing in the mortuary. Thank God, she was alive.

Carol sat by Alice's bed stroking her hair, muttering soothing, encouraging words. 'It wasn't your fault darling. I should have taking more notice. I'm sorry. Everything is going to be all right from now on. You're not to worry. Just rest and get better.'

She heard Marion approach and turned to face her.

Marion resumed her role as a carer. 'It's going to be all right, she's going to live.'

'You knew didn't you? That something was seriously wrong. I bet you're all smug that you got it right.' Carol laid her head on the bed and sobbed. 'How could I have missed it? I'm her mother for God's sake. What sort of parent doesn't know their own child?'

All Marion's anger with her sister evaporated at the sight of her distress. She put her arms around her. 'It's probably no consolation but she didn't tell me anything, I guessed.'

'Well you guessed right and I guessed wrong. Bravo. Aunt Marion, the heroine.'

'We don't know for sure *why* she did it yet. Exams, hormones, boys, they could all be to blame for making her so depressed. Let's wait and see what she says before we go blaming each other. You've had a shock, we all have. It's just that I've seen it all before, here in the hospital. Alice isn't the first child to be brought in as a result of problems at school. They all hide it from their parents, just like Alice kept it a secret from you, from me. She was too afraid of how we would all react if she told us. The main thing is how we deal with it from now on. You're right not to be angry with her. It's not her fault. She must be made to see that.'

Alice's eyes flickered open.

At that moment, her father, Mark, appeared carrying a holder containing two polystyrene cups of coffee. His white shirt creased from travelling. He had taken the first available flight, from Munich to Manchester, early that morning. His patterned paisley tie hung loose and lopsided around his neck. Marion thought he had put on weight and he was definitely greyer.

He placed the coffee on the bedside table feeling tired and flustered. He was an accountant for a multi-national pharmaceutical company, which meant travelling all over the world for meetings. He put the money in the bank and Carol paid the bills on time, stocked the house with food, and took care of Alice and Tom, which she had done a very good job of up to now; before she started working at that damn jewellers shop. But what annoyed him more than that, was his sister-in-law, waiting in the wings, thinking she could do better.

'Alice, darling.' he went to perch on the other side of the bed to Carol and took his daughter's hand. 'My sweet, little girl.'

Alice groaned. 'Mum.'

'I'm right here.' Carol squeezed her other hand.

'Don't try to speak,' Marion told her, 'you've had a tube put down your throat to make you sick; it's bound to be sore for a while.'

She slipped her hand beneath Alice's head and lifting it slightly, held a plastic cup of water to her lips. Alice took a sip; her eyes began to close. Marion released her back down gently on to the pillow. 'She needs to sleep. I'll stay here tonight. I'm sure Sister Harding can put me to good use. I'll call you as soon as there's any news.'

'I'm not leaving her,' Carol insisted.

'Please, go home, both of you. I promise I'll ring first thing in the morning.'

Nobody moved. Paul ran his hands through his hair; he could not cope with all this right now. He wanted a drink, a cold beer or a whisky on the rocks. He did not dare say that though.

'I could do with a shower,' he said.

Carol relented. 'Oh all right. I suppose you know best.'

Sister Harding came to show them out. Carol walked on ahead; Mark hung back. Marion stood at the foot of Alice's bed reading her notes from a blue file. Mark waited until the double doors to the ward had closed behind Carol, before turning to Marion.

'I know Alice is fond of you, but we'll take it from here. She's *our* daughter.'

It was like a stab in her heart when Mark spoke to her. She knew exactly what he was getting at. 'Do you think it matters that's she's not my daughter? Shouldn't you just be concentrating on having everyone around Alice that can help her regardless, even if it means cancelling a few business trips now and again?'

Mark opened his mouth to retaliate but thought better of it. She was right. He had been absent frequently throughout Alice's life including her birth. Marion had helped bring Alice into this world and had been there for her more often than he had.

Marion saw his shoulders sag. She placed the file back into its holder and went to stand in front of him. 'Very often parents can be too close, too intimidating. Alice doesn't want to let you or Carol down, but me... She might not feel like I'm judging her.'

'Just don't do anything without our agreement. Understand?'

Marion understood that he had to have the final say. To him it meant he still had some degree of control over everything.

'I won't,' she assured him.

She watched him leave, concerned. He had every right to shut her out of Alice's life and, the way Carol felt about her close involvement with her niece, she did not doubt her sister would support him.

Alice looked peaceful as she slept; the worst was over. Marion went to find Sister Harding and put herself to good use around the ward whilst she carried out her night vigil.

She became aware that someone was close by and woke up, her neck stiff from having fallen asleep in the chair at the side of Alice's bed; she began to massage it. Daylight streamed in the windows. She wondered what time it was. The only noise piercing the tranquillity surrounded her, was the regular beat of Alice's heart on the monitor. Marion looked over at the nurse changing the drip. 'Jodie!'

'Hey, welcome back,' Jodie said in a hushed voice. 'It's not a nice home coming for you though.'

Marion looked at Alice. 'How is she?'

'Groggy but fine.'

'What are you doing here anyway? I thought you were on the afternoon shifts this week.'

'Susan called me to tell me about Alice.'

'Susan? Oh Sister Harding, I never think she has a name like the rest of us.'

'She said you'd been here all night, so I'm taking over your shift. There's nothing more you can do now except go home and get some more sleep.'

'I need to ring Carol and Richard, let them know.'

'How is Richard now your back?'

'Different. Like he's trying for husband of the year award. To tell you the truth, it's all too much to take in. One minute he can't speak to me civilly, the next he wants to whisk me off on holiday, like the old days, he said.'

Marion was happily coming round to the idea that the old Richard was dead and buried. Instead of feeling hopelessly lost and alone, at last, she felt there was something to look forward to; a future with Richard that at one time she thought she would never have.

'You certainly gave me some good advice when you suggested I go away without him.'

'Did you have a good time in France?'

Even though it seemed like a world wind had occurred since she left France, it had not stopped her thinking about François. She knew from the one and only text he had sent that he had not forgotten her. 'I see you everywhere, most of all in my heart.'

A part of her would always belong to him. Yet, she was beginning to believe she had made the right choice.

'Yes.' She smiled at Jodie. 'I had a lovely time.'

'And what has Richard been up to whilst you were away?'

'Work I presume. I haven't asked.'

So, Richard's blonde secret had stayed with him. It did not sound to Jodie like he was going to tell just yet, if at all.

'Well I can't wait to hear all about it. But first, off you go and get some rest.'

Whilst she waited for the taxi to take her home, Marion made the calls, first to Carol, then Richard.

'I'm sorry I got angry with you,' Carol said. 'Sometimes I feel she'd rather be your daughter than mine.'

'That's just the guilt talking. You mustn't blame yourself. It wasn't your fault.'

Marion arrived home feeling fatigued, the sort that came from relief. Alice was going to be alright. Her whole body wanted to drop somewhere and not move. She forced herself to make some toast and tea and curled up on the sofa to eat it.

She would work with her sister and brother-in-law, if he allowed her, to ensure Alice got all the support she needed. Richard had told her to rest for the day; *he* would do the cooking tonight. She fell asleep dreaming of a beach, a boat and a man. She tried hard to make out his face, but it remained blurred.

25

They kept Alice in for one more night. Marion had forced herself to stay away knowing she was in capable hands with the staff on duty. Besides, it was her parents that belonged by her bedside. Carol told her Alice had said nothing about the incident. All she did was cry. They had not put any pressure on her to tell them why she did it. Her brother Jake was coming home from university for a couple of days in the hope she would open up to him.

The following morning, before her parents arrived to take her home, Marion spent a few minutes with Alice. She appeared distressed, pale, even thinner than the last time Marion had seen her, the afternoon she came for tea.

'Everything will be alright. You'll see. We're all here to help you. You're not alone, whatever the problem.' Marion reassured her.

Alice bit her lip but once again, she failed to stop the tears from cascading down her cheeks. 'I'm sorry,' she sobbed into Marion's shoulder as she held her.

'I think it's us that need to be sorry,' Marion told her. 'We all knew something was wrong. You know, if you can't talk to your mum or dad or even to me, then there are people, professionals, who can help you.'

'There's no point; it'll only make things worse.'

Marion sat on the bed and squeezed Alice's nail chewed hand, noticing the broken skin down the side of the nails that had been bitten so hard, it had bled at one time. 'Please let us help you,' Marion urged.

Alice continued to avoid looking at her aunt but eventually nodded in agreement. 'If I tell Mum and Dad about what's been happening, do you promise you'll be there, Alice pleaded. They won't be angry with me if you're there.'

'Oh Alice, they won't be angry with you at all. I'm certain none of this is your fault but yes, if that's what you want, I'll make sure of it.' No matter what your father says, she thought.

Alice was discharged from hospital. Marion supervised it all and watched with concern as Mark and Carol took their daughter home. She had taken both of them aside into the relatives' room earlier, where she explained that Alice had agreed to talk, but only if she was present. She glanced at Mark expecting him to object.

'Has she told you anything?' he demanded.

Marion shook her head.

Mark reluctantly nodded in agreement. 'We'll phone you when she's ready to talk.'

Marion knew he did not want her there.

Carol phoned her the following day to say Alice had agreed to tell them everything that evening as long as she was present.

Marion arrived at her sister's, holding a large box of Milk Tray. The house, a semi detached, was sandwiched between two steep roads. Everyone parked at the back and entered the house via a small garden path, which led to a large kitchen. Carol had the patience for gardening that Marion lacked. She admired the colourful display of hanging baskets that Carol had arranged along the back wall of the house; they reminded her of the pots and baskets of Geraniums, hanging at Véronique's guesthouse in France. For a moment she was overcome by a feeling of melancholy. She missed her friend. Véronique would have been a great source of support right now; such was her nature.

Marion knocked on the door.

'Why have you brought those?' Carol asked.

'There's nothing in my opinion like chocolate to raise the spirit and we could all do with some of that, especially Alice. Milk Tray are her favourites aren't they?'

'You know they are. You buy her a box every Christmas.'

'Well then, lets hope after tonight that Christmas has come early.'

Alice was curled up on the end of the brown leather sofa, a soft beige chenille throw covered her legs and she hugged a cushion. Carol went to sit on the arm of the sofa, next to her and stroked her hair as if she was an infant. Mark sat in the armchair opposite, which, to Marion's surprise, left a space next to Alice for her. She offered round the box of chocolates as an icebreaker, smiling when Alice took her favourite with the soft strawberry filling.

'So, Alice, what's this all about?' her father asked tentatively, like he needed to know but was scared to finally find out in case he couldn't help his daughter, in case he felt useless.

Alice looked at Marion who simply nodded to encourage her to speak.

'There's this girl at school, called Kelly Morgan.'

Marion heard Carol take a sharp intake of breath. She avoided looking at her.

'Go on,' Mark said gently.

'She's been bullying me.' There, it was out in the open now. Her life would be even less worth living than before. 'You can't go to school and tell them. She'll get angrier with me.'

Mark lent forward as if he was chairing a meeting. 'Just tell us what she's been doing. We'll discuss what we're going to do about it later.'

Alice told them the various things Kelly and her friends had done to punish her for getting better results in class. She told them about the time she had supposedly lost a pencil case. 'Kelly flushed everything down the toilet.' She explained how Kelly had confiscate items of her clothing.

'So that's why I had to keep buying you cardigans,' Carol butted in. 'I never could understand how anyone could lose as many as you did. What about you're other friends?'

'They kept their distance; they were frightened she'd turn on them and start calling them names, teasing them like she did me.'

'Oh! My poor baby.' Carol kissed her daughter's head and hugged her. She looked at her husband. He had sat back in his chair as if he was taking in all the facts, like the businessman he was, before coming to his decision. 'Did she ever hit you?' he said.

Alice shook her head. 'She threatened to. She told me to be outside the school one day at four o'clock. She did it on purpose to frighten me. When that day came, she told me she'd changed her mind, she wasn't going to risk getting expelled and would find another way to get rid of me. I was so scared of what she would think up to do next. That's why I…' Alice began to cry.

Marion put her arm around her, not caring what Mark thought about it. 'Well done. You deserve to eat all of these,' and handed her the box of chocolates.

Alice smiled through her tears.

'I'll put the kettle on.' Carol disappeared into the kitchen before her own tears became visible.

'Right!' Mark said. 'This is what we're going to do. First, I want a meeting with the headmaster. I want to know what he intends to do about bullying in his school. I want this Kelly expelled. Secondly…'

'Secondly, I'll kick her head in; no one bullies my little sister and gets away with it.'

Mark spun round to see his tall, blond son striking the pose of a typical geeky student with his newly acquired glasses.

Alice's face lit up. 'Jake!' She squealed, jumped off the sofa, almost tripping over the throw as she ran to him. She had never been so grateful to see her older brother as she was at that moment. She threw her arms around his neck.

'Hey!' He peeled her off him gently, embarrassed at the outward show of emotion. 'Mum's just filled me in on it all. I think I may be able to solve the problem. I know Darren, Kelly's older brother, he's cool. I'll have a word, he's always bragging how he can get Kelly to do anything for him. Claims she puts him on a pedestal. I know the feeling.' He laughed, looking at Alice.

She could not care how much Jake teased her, she was so happy to have him there. Nevertheless, she could not resist a dig herself.

'Just who came rushing back when he found out *his* sister was in trouble? I'd say that shows you think a lot about me as well.'

Jake smiled. 'Nah, I just knew I was the one to sort it all out. What would you do without me, eh sis?' He gave her a friendly punch on the arm. 'You'll have no problems once Darren has finished with his sister.'

Whilst this happy reunion was taking place, Mark felt a little put out that his son had stolen his thunder, just when he thought he had it all under control. However, he could not fault Jake's proposed solution to it all. He could do with someone pragmatic like that amongst his board of directors; they were full of hot air most of them. Not wanting to relinquish total control of the situation, after all he was the man of the house, he said 'Well that's great Jake, but I still want to speak to the headmaster.'

'Please Dad, let's just wait and see if Jake's idea works first. You're not going to help me if Kelly sees you arriving at school for a meeting with the head.'

'She shouldn't even be allowed to stay at the school after what she's done.'

'But you can't get all her friends expelled, what if they simply carry on after Kelly leaves?'

'She's right Mark; one thing at a time.' Carol brought in a tray, balancing five mugs of tea. She would have brought out a plate of custard creams, Alice's favourite, if Marion had not brought the chocolates. She beamed from ear to ear because her son was home. All the family were together, just as it should be when there was a crisis to deal with.

Marion looked at the happy reunion with a tinge of sadness. Carol really was the lucky one. She saw no need to stay once she had finished her tea; this problem would resolve itself without her help. She would just have to be content with looking forward to inviting Alice to tea again very soon, so she could hear all about it.

Carol followed Marion to the door.

'You do know who Kelly Morgan is, don't you?' Carol said when they were both out of earshot.

'No.' Marion answered her. 'Should I?'

'Richard's boss, what's his name? Paul Morgan. It's his daughter.'

26

Marion was fuming. She cursed under her breath all the way home from her sister's house. 'All those times I listened to Sandra going on about how perfect her children were, I bet she doesn't know the half of it.' She could not wait to tell Richard.

He was in bed when she arrived home. Mimi raised her head from the cushion Marion had taken to leaving for her on the kitchen chair. She stopped to give the cat a quick tickle behind the ears before rushing upstairs.

Richard smiled as she entered the bedroom; he saw the look of thunder on her face. She repeated what Carol had told her. 'You need to tell him; tell your boss to stop his daughter from bullying Alice. I can't believe it.'

'And you expect me to sort all this out?'

'He's your boss. You have to do something to help Alice; now you know what that horrible girl has done to her. Besides, Carol and Mark will expect you to say something.'

'And just how am I supposed to do that and still have a job?'

'He can't fire you for telling him the truth about his daughter. She's a bully and she needs to be stopped.'

'I thought you said Jake had it all under control? Can't we wait and see what happens before I get involved?'

'No!' Marion's eyes clouded over.

'It's not my place Marion, if anything, it's up to Mark.'

'Alice could have died.'

Richard sighed. He had enough going on in his life to worry about without this. Somehow, he knew he was not going to win this argument with Marion. 'Alright.'

Marion sat down on the edge of the bed next to him. He slipped his arm around her and gave her a gentle squeeze. 'I'll think of someway of slipping it into the conversation.'

'This isn't the time to be subtle, Richard. Try... my niece tried to kill herself thanks to your daughter. That should get his attention.'

Richard left for work the next day, knowing he had two choices. He could either say something to Paul or keep quiet and lie to Marion. He was already and expert at the latter.

Paul appeared to be in good spirits when Richard arrived at the depot. He beamed at Richard as he came through the door of his office. 'What a weekend; two under par. My best score yet on the golf course.'

'Well done.' Richard forced a smile.

'How was your weekend?' he asked Richard, whilst shuffling papers around on his desk.

Richard took a deep breath. 'Not good.'

Paul stopped shuffling and looked up. 'Oh! Why's that?'

Richard's heart beat quickened. Marion had been right; Alice could have died. Still, he could not believe he had agreed to do this.

'Marion's niece took an overdose. She's fine now,' he said quickly. But she had to spend a night in hospital.'

'Do you know why she did it?'

Here goes my job, thought Richard. 'Alice, Marion's niece, told the family she had been bullied.' He could not look at Paul, 'by your daughter.'

He wanted to run. Paul sat down in his oversized, red leather chair and began to swivel from side to side. An angry expression crept across his face.

'Come and sit down Richard.'

Richard obeyed him. He perched upright in the wooden carver chair on the opposite side of the desk to Paul.

'Why do you think I offered you the Directors post?'

'Is this the bit where I say because I'm good at my job? Then you surprise me with some other reason.'

'Directors are busy people; they often have to work late, they are required to come into the depot at the drop of hat because there is a problem, even if there isn't...' Paul tapped the side of his nose. 'I did you a favour and now you're going to do me one.'

'What do you mean?' Richard said.

Paul smiled. 'Does Marion know you've been playing away from home?'

Richard's heart began to thump. 'I'm not.'

If he thought he could deflect Paul's suspicion, he was wrong.

'I have eyes and ears in the solicitors next door that tell me otherwise.'

Richard frowned, then realised what Paul meant. 'These eyes and ears, do they belong to a tall, thin man with a big nose?'

Paul laughed. 'I suppose by telling me, he hoped I would put a stop to it by telling Marion. Which, of course I could still do.'

Richard's stomach turned. 'Why would you do that?'

Paul lent forward over the desk. 'My daughter is not a bully and I don't care for your accusations that she is.'

'Okay. There's no need to shoot the messenger,' Richard said.

'Let's hope not. If you have to play the role of errand boy, you had better tell Marion not to pursue this any further or she'll end up with more than she bargained for.

Now, shall we get back to the more important business of running this place?'

Richard took that as a dismissal and vacated Paul's office. He avoided his boss as much as he could for the rest of the day, deciding it was better to let the dust settle than to keep churning it up.

It was his night to cook. He stopped off at the supermarket on his way home and bought what he needed to make chicken chasseur, a recipe he had watched one of those TV chefs prepare. To compliment the dish, he chose a bottle of Sauvignon Blanc. Whilst he wondered around, he found himself thinking how many of the men he saw were having an affair. How many ended up with a pregnant mistress? Forced to either agree to an abortion to keep their wives, or lose the wife and keep the child. It sent chills down his spine.

When he arrived home, Marion was already running a bath.

'I've bought a Sauvignon,' he shouted upstairs. 'It needs chilling. I'll just put it in the freezer for a few minutes then I'll bring you a glass.'

He emptied the food out of the carrier bag, helped himself to a beer from the fridge and set too, slicing the mushrooms. He cut up an onion, put a knob of butter in a pan, seasoned two chicken breasts and lowered them into the melted butter to brown. Exactly how he had seen the chef do it on TV. By which time, he considered the wine cold enough to take Marion a glass.

The bathroom smelt of grapefruit, one of her many assortments of bath oils, to which she often treated herself.

Marion took the glass from him. 'Did you say something to Paul?'

'Yes and I wish I hadn't.'

'Why?'

'He's denying it all. His precious daughter is not a bully. Look Marion; leave me out of this. Alice is only my niece by marriage and you're doing it again; acting as if she's your daughter. This is Carol and Mark's battle not yours.'

Marion sipped her wine and looked at Richard. 'Can Paul really make things awkward for you now that you've spoken out?'

'More than you could ever think,' he said, nervously.

'Alright. At least he's aware. We'll have to wait and see. But if Alice continues to be bullied…'

Richard left the bathroom, shutting the door behind him. He leant against it and closed his eyes as the smell of burning chicken drifted up the stairs. He prayed that the whole business of Alice and Paul's daughter would resolve itself without Marion. He could not warn her that if she persisted in getting involved she was going to end up with the biggest shock of her life.

27

The late afternoon sun burnt through the windows; the school bus became a greenhouse. Alice willed the driver to get a move on before she melted. She wished she had walked home; she could have bought an ice pop from the newsagents.

Kelly and her two stooges sat four rows in front of her. Alice automatically raised her hand to her mouth and chewed on her nails. She could not break the habit, like sucking her thumb when she was younger. To stop her from doing it, her mum had put some fowl tasting liquid on it.

Even though Jake had been true to his word and had spoken to Kelly's brother about the bullying, she still became nervous when Kelly was around. These days, Kelly simply glared at her with hatred. Alice believed that if looks could kill, she would have died many times over by now.

Sometimes, she had caught the three of them in class, crammed together staring at her, whispering and laughing. Without Jake permanently here to fight her corner, it was like waiting for a ticking time bomb to explode. When that day came, she vowed she would run and run and run. She could not face it all again.

Apart from the headmaster, nobody knew at the school about Alice's attempt at suicide. Alice's father wanted Kelly out of his daughter's life for good. He wanted to have her expelled or to move Alice to another school. Alice did not want either. Providing Kelly stayed away from her she did not want to change schools. How long would it take to make new friends? If every school had a Kelly, Jake was not likely to know their brother.

When the bus finally pulled away, everyone let out sighs of relief. Alice continued to stare out of the window, clutching her school bag on her knee. The closeness of it to her body made her even hotter and she began to feel agitated. She still had twenty more minutes to endure before she could get off.

The bus wound its way through housing estates until finally, it was Alice's stop next. She began to make her way down the aisle to stand at the door ready. As she passed, Kelly swivelled sideways in her seat, blocking Alice's route with her junky legs. Her feet appeared enormous in bulky white combos.

Alice's heart jumped.

'Going somewhere?' Kelly sneered.

'Let me pass,' Alice said, almost in a whisper.

'I think you've missed the magic word. Did you hear it girls?' She turned to her army of two and they all laughed. Alice looked up in earnest to see if the driver had seen what was going on in his mirror; he seemed oblivious to the commotion. The bus turned into the end of Alice's street. If she did not reach the door, the driver would presume no one wanted to get off, and he would drive on to the next stop. Those close by were aware of what was happening and stared at Alice. She was embarrassed, her cheeks were hot and flushed. She felt like she was suffocating. She had to get off the bus out into the cooler air.

'Well. We're waiting.' Kelly sniped. 'Tut! Tut! Fancy being so impolite. We really can't have that, can we girls?'

Alice could feel the panic rising up. She needed to run. Kelly was far too big to push out of the way so Alice did the only thing she could think of; lifting her arm, she slapped Kelly across the face. She heard the scream but had already jumped over Kelly's legs and was hurtling down the bus towards the front door. The driver almost had to make an emergency stop. Alice jumped off and ran home as fast as she could without looking back. She heard the engine as the bus pulled away, and was flooded with relief. No one was coming after her. She arrived home crimson and breathless.

'You haven't been running in this heat? Carol asked her daughter. 'You're mad!'

She got Alice a glass of water, which she gulped down in one. She slumped, into a chair, her breathing still laboured from her dash to freedom.

Ever since the suicide attempt, Carol had watched Alice anxiously. She was aware of the still bitten fingernails and could not stop asking leading questions like: 'How has your day been? Are your friends alright?' She needed to make sure Alice was not deceiving her. She had made such a good job of it last time and she, Alice's mum, had made an even better job of presuming her daughter's unhappiness was down to hormones or boys. If there was the slightest hint that Alice was miserable, for whatever reason, she wanted to know. Moreover, if it were because of a boy, life would be perfectly normal.

Before she could ask this time, Alice pre-empted her. 'I got 19/20 for my maths test and I slapped Kelly Morgan across the face.'

Marion was laughing on the phone when Richard walked in the door. Mimi scurried passed him to get outside before he shut it. She put her hand over the phone and mouthed to Richard, 'Alice has slapped Kelly across the face.'

Richard could feel the colour drain from him. He wanted to know if Alice had apologised, when his phone beeped with a message from Clare. She was on her way over to the house.

'Oh for God's sake!' He cursed under his breath and disappeared outside again to phone her. He walked down the drive, waiting for her to answer. When she did, he yelled, 'What the hell do you think your doing? You can't come here, not now.'

Out of the corner of his eye, he saw a man with a black mongrel dog, approaching the house. As he passed, he nodded at Richard; the dog growled at him because he was shouting. Undeterred, Richard continued. 'You just can't show up like that.'

'Why? Are you and Marion having a cosy night together? I'm sure she'd be interested in what I have to say.'

His mistress wanted to meet his wife and tell all…great! If Marion did not hear it from Clare, she was probably going to hear it from Paul, thanks to Alice. He felt like a snared animal.

'Meet me at the pub, I'll say, its work and I've got to go out.' He stormed back up the drive to the house.

Marion met him with a barrage of questions. 'Why did you go outside? Who was on the phone?'

He went straight to the bottom of the stairs and retrieved his jacket without answering her.

'Now where are you going?'

'I've got to go out. There's a problem at the depot.'

'Why doesn't Paul take care of it? It's his business. He's clearly not busy sorting his daughter out!'

'How do I know,' Richard snapped.

He could not do this anymore. He saw the look of astonishment on Marion's face. 'I'll try not to be too long,' he said, more calmly.

At the pub, Clare sat in the corner away from everyone, sipping Perrier water. He sat down next to her.

'You can save your breath,' she snapped at him. 'I'm having an abortion. If you're not going to stand by me, I'm getting rid of it. I'm making an appointment for next week.'

He nodded, accepting her patience was wearing thin, the clock was ticking and his time was up.

He had done everything Marion had asked of him on her return from France. He wanted to be the good, caring husband. If only he had not been so stupid. One minute Marion was discussing with him about changing the wallpaper and buying new furniture; now she was about to learn he was leaving her for another woman who was having his baby. It was his duty. It was not what he wanted. It would crucify Marion.

He laid his hand on Clare's swollen stomach; she covered it with her own. He noticed her French manicured nails. Even in a time of crisis, her appearance remained important. He liked that about her. He entwined his fingers in hers. 'There's no need to make the appointment.'

28

Marion felt herself drifting off to sleep on the sofa whilst she waited for Richard to come back from the depot. Finally, she gave in to the exhaustion and went to bed. Sleeping deeply, she did not hear him come home.

The sun, creeping around the edge of the curtains, woke her. She stretched her legs out down the bed, rolled over and saw the empty space. The covers showed no signs of being disturbed and her stomach lurched. She knew from experience how treacherous the Motorway between Huddersfield and Leeds could be by day, and even more so, in the dark. Her mind began to relay thoughts that something awful had happened.

She threw on her dressing gown and raced downstairs. Richard was not in the kitchen. When she saw his car keys on the table, relief flooded through her; at least he had made it home. She found him in the living room, sat on the sofa.

An enlarged, framed wedding photograph of them holding hands and looking into each other's eyes hung on the opposite wall. It was a snap shot of a moment in time when they had been truly happy. Richard stared at it.

'What time did you get back?' Marion asked him. 'Why didn't you come to bed?'

Richard kept his eyes on the picture. 'It rained the day we got married, some say it's a bad omen when that happens.' He spoke as if in a trance. 'It means the marriage won't last.' He turned to look at her, his eyes, wet and bloodshot.

She sat down beside him and placed her hand on his knee. 'What's happened? Why are you talking like that?'

Richard pulled her close and held her. Instinctively she slipped her arms around his neck. 'Richard you're frightening me, what's wrong?'

He hesitated for a moment. 'I've been lying to you,' he said.

She tensed. She wanted to pull away from him but he clung to her, holding her even tighter.

'I don't understand. Why?'

'I did something stupid. I'm so sorry.'

'What? What did you do Richard? For God's sake, what are you trying to tell me?

He broke away from her and stood by the window; that way, he did not have to look into her eyes and see the pain of what he was about to tell her. He watched as cars left their driveways, most likely for the weekly trip to the supermarket. It was just another normal Saturday morning for most people; there was nothing normal about it for him.

Marion stared after him, her heart racing.

'After Anna died,' he said softly, 'you let the grief swallow you up. It was as if I ceased to exist.'

'That's not true.' Marion protested.

'Let's just say it felt like it. I needed you. But you weren't there.' He faltered.

Marion saw his shoulders rise and heard him take a deep breath.

Placing his hands on the window ledge, Richard hung his head. 'I had an affair. Her name is Clare.' He closed his eyes. 'She's pregnant.'

Something invisible hit Marion in the stomach. She fought to get her breath.

He turned round and took a step towards her with his arms outstretched. 'I never meant for any of it to happen. If I could take it all back I would, believe me. I'm so sorry.'

Marion jumped up and moved away from him. Her heart thumped hard against her chest. 'Why?' She glared at him. 'Because I couldn't give you a child, you decided to find somebody else to get one.'

'It wasn't like that.'

'Just what was it like?'

'I didn't set out to have an affair.'

She flung her arms in the air. 'I suppose she just threw herself at you and you couldn't resist.'

Her heart was beating so fast she felt breathless. 'When did it start?'

He could not look at her. 'March, April. I can't remember. I ended it when you went to France.'

He said the words as if he considered it a peace offering.

'I went to France in the hope it would save our marriage. I needn't have bothered; it was already over.'

The exasperation and anger spilled out of her. She launched herself at him, thumping, slapping, his chest, his arms; tears stung her eyes. 'You bastard! Bastard! Bastard!' With each hit, she screamed the word.

Richard did nothing to stop her. Finally, she gave up, spent of emotion. She dropped her hands and glared at him with hatred.

'I never stopped loving you, Marion. But you were so wrapped up…'

'You're actually blaming *me* for the reason you had an affair. Whilst I struggled to deal with it all, you got your comfort by jumping into bed with a complete stranger.'

'Yes, if you have to look at it that way; she was a relief from it all. You couldn't stop thinking about anything else. You chose to ignore that fact that I was still around. It felt like you blamed me for Anna's death. You couldn't bear to come near me.'

'So you held some sort of angry grudge.'

'Now you're being childish.'

'Well how do you explain it? Anyway, you have what you wanted now. I presume she's keeping the baby or you wouldn't have to come clean and admitted it all to me.'

The reality began to sink in for Marion. Her throat constricted as she forced to control the tears forming in place of the anger. She lifted her head high and squared her shoulders. 'So you're going to be a father,' she said sarcastically. 'Congratulations.'

She fled the room and ran upstairs, curling up into a ball on the bed, she wrapped her arms around herself; her body shook as she sobbed. Her chest felt so tight, as though it would burst. Surely, she was allowed to grieve for as long as it took. If she had pushed Richard away, she had not been aware, nor had she done it deliberately, so why did he feel the need to have an affair? Why had he not talked to her?

Feeling cold from the shock, she pulled the duvet over her shaking body and sobbed for a short while longer. Eventually, her body calmed itself. She lay, taking short, sniffling breaths. The duvet cover beneath her face was sodden. Slowly, she sat up and reached for a tissue from the box on the bedside table. She wiped her face, blew her nose and heaved herself off the bed to stand in front of the window. The glass was smeared with old raindrops. Every morning when she opened the curtains, she was reminded of the need to clean them. That job was still on the 'to do' list, and would most likely remain there now. As she looked out, the sun played hide and seek with the clouds. Anger swelled up inside her once more but she was exhausted; it had lost its strength compared to before. How could he do this to her? The same questions were on a repeat loop inside her head because she had no answers to them.

Richard's slow, muffled footsteps sounded on the stairs. She knew exactly where he was; the second to last stair tread always creaked.

Her stubborn pride took over; she wiped away the remaining tears with a fresh tissue.

Richard walked into the bedroom carrying two mugs. 'I've made some tea.' He put a mug down on the table at the side of her, stealing a glance at her red, swollen eyes. He sat on the end of the bed.

Marion reached for the mug, she felt like throwing the tea at him. Instead, she took a sip; the hot liquid penetrated her body, soothing her dry throat. She sat back down on the bed as far away from him as she could, her shoulders slumped; his confession had crushed her. She bit her lip in an effort to prevent more tears.

Silence hung between them.

Marion was the first to speak. She gripped the handle of the mug, her voice quivered, 'I want to know everything from the beginning. I want to know why you did it. How old she is. What she looks like.'

Richard took a sip of his tea, whilst he gathered his thoughts. 'Are you sure you want to hear all this?'

Marion sniffed and nodded.

'She's twenty six, small with blonde hair. She came over to talk to me in the pub one night. I bought her a drink and we chatted for a while. I saw her again, a couple of times in the same bar, but she always came over to me, not the other way round. I wasn't looking for anyone else. I know you don't believe me, but it's true. It just happened.'

Strangely, Marion did believe him. It happened exactly like that between her and François. She did not go to France to find love; it found her, when she needed it.

'There was such a void between us. When you decided to go to France on your own, I guess that's when I came to my senses. I ended it.'

She swung round to face him. 'And came crawling back to me with your promises.'

'I was all set to come and surprise you in France. I hoped you might see it as a romantic gesture. Then Clare turned up at the house and told me she was pregnant. Since it was over between us, it was natural to suggest she had an abortion, she threaten to, but every time she talked about it, I thought of Anna. How can I ask her to get rid of a baby deliberately? You can understand that. Can't you?'

'So, she wants to keep it.'

Richard looked away from her and sighed heavily. 'Only if I'm part of the package.'

Marion placed the mug on the bedside table. Keeping her stare fixed on the soaked tissue in her hand she breathed in. 'Do you want to be?'

'Shouldn't the question be do I want to live with the knowledge that given a choice I chose to end the life of my child? No, is the answer to that.'

'Anna would have been born into a loving relationship. You haven't once said you love this Clare. Do you?'

He resumed looking at her. 'Not in the way I love you.'

'If we'd have gone on to have another child we wouldn't be in this mess,' she said. 'It all keeps coming back to being my fault.' Her head dropped into her hands and her shoulder's shook. The sobs grew louder.

Richard placed his half-full mug of cold tea on the dressing table and moved to put his arm around her. He felt her stiffen but he left it there. 'It's both our faults,' he said gently.

Marion wiped her eyes with the wet tissue.

'It's ironic.' She sniffed. 'What we both needed was right here, if we'd just talked to each other. Instead we turned to someone else.'

He stared at her. 'What do you mean, *we*?'

All Marion's intentions of keeping quiet about François disappeared at that moment. It was the natural response to want to hit back after Richard's revelations.

When she had finished, he removed his arm from around her shoulders and stood by the window. His raised hands were clasped tightly behind his head as if he was going to lunge forward and punch the window with them. She waited for him to say something, daring him even. When he did not, she knew what she had to do.

'I think I should meet Clare.'

He spun round. 'Why? What are you going to do?'

'I'm not going to get into a cat fight with her, if that's what you think. I just want to talk to her, without you. You'd better give me her phone number.'

*

The following morning, Paul called Richard into his office. He stood with his hands on the desk, his large frame leaning over it like a predator about to strike its prey.

Richard was not in the mood to play cat and mouse.

'If this is about Alice you can save your breath. Marion knows everything. And for the record I don't know how you can sleep at night knowing what your daughter is responsible for.'

He walked out, slamming the office door behind him.

29

The phone call to Clare took three attempts. Marion picked up the phone the first time, putting it down again without dialling the number. What was the point of a conversation? Richard had made his bed...he would have to move in with his pregnant mistress. But if he still loved her, as he had said, this was all about the baby, not Clare.

The second time, she got as far as dialling the number before putting the phone down again after two rings. What was she supposed to say to this woman? 'Hello I'm Richard's wife, what do you think you're up to?' She was big enough to acknowledge that, although Clare was guilty of seducing her husband, she would not have succeeded had Richard not been willing.

On the third attempt, Clare answered after just one ring. 'Hello!' A confident, cheery voice sounded in Marion's ear. Caught off guard, Marion was unable to speak, her heart pounded in her chest.

'Hello! Richard is that you?'

At the mention of her husband's name, Marion found her voice. 'No. It's Richard's wife,' she replied with anger, feeling pleased to have delivered the shock.

There was a brief silence before Clare responded. 'Richard said you would be ringing.'

He had warned her. The two of them were as thick as thieves. Marion felt betrayed. Was there any reason why she should continue with this folly? Except that she could hardly back down now.

'I think we should meet and talk about all of this.' She held her breath, expecting Clare to resist, after all why would she want to meet the wife when she was only interested in the husband. To Marion's surprise, Clare was quite amenable.

'Alright. Where do you suggest?'

They agreed to meet at the White Rose shopping centre, conveniently situated between Leeds and Huddersfield.

Clare was not what Marion expected. The woman standing in front of her was no ordinary small blonde as Richard had described. She wore a plain pink shift dress that suited her neat compact frame. Marion's eyes fleetingly surveyed her stomach; it showed only a hint of the pregnancy. The slight height of the kitten heeled white sandals she wore on her tanned feet accentuated her shapely calf muscles, and her hair hung in a neat, straight bob framing her unlined face. She wore the minimum of make up, some black mascara that made her baby blue eyes striking and a hint of pink lipstick. She did not need any more; her skin had captured the bloom of pregnancy. She looked young, fresh, chic and beautiful. Marion felt all of her forty years.

As Marion approached, Clare stood proud, like 'the cat that got the cream'. The confidence Marion had heard over the phone oozed from every pore of her physique. Marion felt instantly like she was starting on the back foot, very much the spurned wife. She would have to find the strength from somewhere to turn this around. She was not going to be out manoeuvred by a woman almost half her age.

They sat at a table in Costa Coffee, in the back corner, out of the way of eavesdroppers. Aromatic waves of filtered coffee infused the air. Marion glanced at the woman Richard had taken to bed. He could not have picked someone more different in looks. A tall red head verses a small blonde.

Marion nursed a strong black coffee. Something she had learnt to like in France. There it had been *un double espresso*. Clare had gone for the more healthy option of green tea. She spoke first.

'Why did you want to meet?'

Marion stared her straight in the eye. 'Why did you seduce my husband?'

Clare laughed. 'Is that what he told you?'

Marion glanced around to see if anyone was listening, they all seemed to be engrossed in there own conversations.

'Does it really matter who started it? It happened and I'm having his baby. Isn't that really why you're here?

Marion's eyes pricked with tears. She had underestimated Clare's strong character, and her own weakness in dealing with such an emotionally charged encounter.

Clare apologised. 'That sounded horrible. Richard told me about the baby you lost.'

'Of course he has. And I suppose he told you how I refused to try for another and how he always blamed me.'

'No. He didn't say any of that. Perhaps the only person who blames yourself is you. On the other hand, if you hadn't neglected him he wouldn't have felt the need to reach out to me. Maybe that's what you should be feeling guilty about, and I should thank you for.'

Marion had told Richard she did not want a catfight but, at this moment, all she wanted to do was scratch Clare's eyes out. Apart from the obvious, she could not understand what had attracted Richard to her.

Marion composed herself by sipping her coffee. 'Do you love Richard?' she asked. 'He told me he ended the affair when he realised he couldn't leave me. Why then are you keeping the baby?'

'You think I'm doing this to trap him.'

'Well, are you?'

Clare's face softened; Marion noticed a sudden shift in her demeanour. Gone was the arrogance she had displayed earlier.

Clare picked up her teaspoon and toyed with it. 'Richard and I… well lets say we never really had any heart to hearts. There were no 'tell me all about yourself' evenings. He doesn't know my mum raised me as a single parent because my dad was an alcoholic and buggered off when I was six months old. This may not mean anything to you, but I don't want the same for my child.' She raised her eyes to look at Marion. 'I gave Richard a choice before it was too late. Be a father or I would have an abortion. Unless he's changed his mind, he chose me and our baby.'

'That still doesn't answer my question. Do you love him?'

'Very much. I loved him from the first day I saw him, which was long before we met in the pub. We met twice, sometimes three times a week at lunch time, queuing for our burgers.' She smiled at the recollection. 'I know what you're thinking. Richard will never love me in the same way. Maybe you're right. But it's hard to stop loving someone just because they don't love you. And remember, he made his choice out of his own free will.'

'No he didn't. You blackmailed him emotionally. You must see that. He can't intentionally agree to end the pregnancy after what we went through.'

'I've given him a second chance and he's taken it. This is our time, Richard's and mine. It would suit you wouldn't it, if I lost this baby as well? Then, it would be me having to face up to losing Richard instead of you.' Clare made a move to stand up. 'I don't think there's anything left to say to each other, do you?'

Marion remained calm. 'Just one thing, abortion is normally refused after twenty four weeks unless there are exceptional circumstances. How can you be sure Richard won't change his mind after that?'

Clare glared at her, swung her handbag onto her shoulder and stormed off.

Marion watched her disappear out of sight, feeling slightly better at having left Clare with that conundrum.

Although she had finished her coffee long ago, she was reluctant to leave the gentle hubbub of conversation, clanging of crockery and gushing noise from the coffee maker. They all reminded her she was not alone, not here in this café anyway.

She had stupidly expected Clare to say she did not really want Richard; she only needed him to support her and the baby. Marion had already thought this through. She would have forgiven the affair, how could she not after France; learned from it even, if it meant that Richard stayed with her. She would not object to how ever much involvement Clare wanted him to have from a distance. Weekly outings, weekends, school holidays, whatever it took, she would be accommodating. But there was no going back now. She had it all wrong. Clare loved him. Clare wanted him to be with her and she was the one having his baby.

She stumbled back to the car, her legs heavy, her vision blurred with tears. She was shaking so much she dropped her car keys whilst fumbling to insert them into the lock. Inside the car, she rested her head on the steering wheel and sobbed. Her marriage was over.

Her mobile rang. 'How did it go?' Jodie asked softly.

'I'm losing my husband to a pretty bitch. Isn't that how it always is?' Marion told her between sobs.

She imagined Clare had relayed to Richard every minute detail by now; how she had made it quite clear he was hers for the taking.

With a heavy heart, she searched in her handbag for a tissue and cleaned the streaked mascara from around her eyes. There was no point in prolonging the inevitable. If she was going to have to pick herself up from this she might as well start sooner than later.

Somehow, she managed to drive home through the mist of continuous tears.

30

Richard took most of his belongings at Marion's request whilst she was at work. She did not want to have to face him. It never occurred to her to change the locks afterwards. When he opened the door and walked in a week later to collect the last of his clothes, he gave her a fright.

'I left some things, I'll just…' He skulked upstairs before Marion could say anything. When he returned, Marion stood in the kitchen, her arms folded, watching him struggle to close the zip on his bulging holdall. She still could not believe this was happening. There was nothing she could do to stop it; even if she wanted to.

Richard gave up trying with the holdall. He pleaded with her. 'Please don't let it end like this.'

'What do you expect? A party?'

'Of course not. This is nothing to celebrate.'

'You're damn right its not but you'll have reason enough to crack open the champagne in five months time. Well I shan't be raising a glass to you.'

'I don't know what to say, except I'm sorry; I never wanted any of this.'

She threw her arms up in the air. 'Don't use that word you don't know the meaning of it,' she cried.

'And what about you and this French man? You're not as innocent as you make out.'

Marion was furious. How could he even begin to compare what she had with Françoise to what he had done with Clare?

'Well I won't be apologising because I know I don't mean it. I'm not sorry for having two of the best weeks of my life with a man who truly cared for me. My one regret now was that I chose to come back to you instead of staying with him.'

She whispered under her breath, 'Now I've lost you both.'

Sighing, she said, 'Just leave will you.'

Richard picked up the holdall, tucked it under his arm to avoid losing any of its contents, opened the door with his free hand and slammed it behind him.

He was gone, out of her life, just like that. She dropped into a chair and brought her hands up to her face. As the tears fell, it was hard not to feel sorry for herself. She had gone from feeling low, to feeling happy and back to low in such a short time. Just when she thought she had finally stopped grieving for Anna, her marriage had ended.

She pulled herself together, made a cup of tea and took it outside. The whole country was basking in an Indian summer. She sat on a wooden bench on the stone patio at the back of the house; her body warmed by the sun gradually began to relax. Mimi appeared with a thin tail hanging out of her mouth, stopping in front of Marion, she dropped her present. Stunned, the mouse shivered before attempting its escape. To Marion's amusement, Mimi had to chase after it.

On the eve of the Millennium, they had had a party at the house to celebrate and had stood on the patio drinking Champagne, watching all the celebratory firework displays across Huddersfield and beyond. It had been a magical evening and they had toasted the new century with hope in their hearts. Now, she sat on the very same spot, feeling alone, lost and resentful, not knowing if she would ever get over Richard's betrayal.

There was no one to fill the empty space beside her in bed, no one to break the silence that surrounded her in every room like an invisible mist. There was now a space where Richard's numerous shirts used to hang, and the shelves, once piled high with his multicoloured t-shirts and jumpers were bare. His bedside drawer, she knew to be full of memorabilia he could not bare to part with, was also empty. She wondered if he had bagged it up as a keepsake of their years together and taken it all with him, or if he had decided, it was time to get rid of it, and start a new collection of mementos of his life with Clare. She had not even come across an odd sock, wedged somewhere and forgotten over time. It was as if he had never lived there.

To avoid spending evenings on her own, Marion had begun working regular night shifts. She had not considered divorce until Carol had surprisingly been so insistent she did. This was the sister, who had thought the sun shone out of Richard. Who could not understand why Marion had left him behind when she went to France.

'What a bastard!' she cried. 'You're surely never going to forgive him so there's no need to stay married. Leave him to his blonde bimbo. You can do much better.'

Marion was amused by her change of heart. She did not want to imagine what her response would be if she told her about François, who she concluded, was bound to have found someone else by now. Whoever it was, she was a lucky woman to have such an attractive, caring man. It would have been her had she known what Richard was doing. Well, she had blown that opportunity. Véronique had sent her an e-mail some time ago; she remembered searching for news of François, and being disappointed that there had been no mention of him.

He would have forgotten all about her by now.

31

At the weekend, the clocks went back; it seemed permanently dark and depressing. Marion had decided that working the night shift had served its purpose these last few weeks when she could not bear being on her own in the house. However, if she was to move on from Richard, she needed a social life, and she was not going to get one by permanently working in the evenings.

Today was her first morning back on the day roster. It was also her birthday.

The day before, Richard had sent her a bouquet of flowers through *Interflora*. She did not understand why he had sent them. It was such an outlandish gesture. It angered her, knowing he used to buy her flowers when he had loved her; all they meant now was a show of his guilt. She took them to work to brighten up the ward, telling everyone, they were from an anonymous donor.

When she arrived at the hospital, the nurses from the night shift had begun their debriefing. In one of the beds, an elderly woman was crying softly to herself. Marion went over and squeezed her un-bandaged hand. She saw from her notes, she had sprained her wrist in a fall. She also had dementia.

More people were arriving into triage by the minute. Each time she picked up a blue patient file from the pile on the desk, it was replaced by another.

The dementia patient was shouting now; she needed the toilet. Marion knew she could not ignore her or she would soil the bed. She looked for someone to help her, but all the other nurses were busy dealing with their own patients; it was tempting to pull rank on one of the juniors, but that would mean taking them away from someone else. She sighed, realising she would have to deal with it. 'I won't be a minute,' she told her.

By ten o' clock, she was desperate for a coffee. There had been no time to drink the one that had been made for her earlier and was now luke warm; she gulped it down. She had not eaten since six that morning, except for a digestive biscuit that Jodie had given her, she began to feel light-headed. If she did not eat soon she might faint and become a patient herself.

Sister Harding caught up with her and wished her happy birthday.

'We're going out for a drink after work, would you like to come?' Marion asked, knowing she had put Sister Harding on the spot, but determined not to leave her out. Her husband had left with another woman; there should be some kind of solidarity after all.

'Please.' Marion insisted. 'I really would like you to join us. We divorced women should stick together.'

'So it's happened then? The Sister said.

'Almost, I sign the decree nisi next week.'

'And how do you feel about that?'

Marion took a deep breath; there were times when her eyes filled with tears and she had to distract herself from crying. 'I'm sad of course and resentful but in a strange way, I'm relieved. I'm forty-one today. What is it they say? Life begins at forty. So what if I am a little late, better that than not at all.'

'In that case, perhaps its time I got out of the starting blocks as well. I'd love to come out later.'

Marion tried not to think how she was going to get through the rest of the shift. She was fatigued already and longed to put her feet up. Her legs ached and her eyelids felt heavy; her body had not become used to working in daylight hours. Roll on tonight, she thought, I'm going to need that drink.

It was almost dark when the three women crossed the road, arms linked, making there way to *The Old Wire Works.* They walked briskly, each shivered against the damp November air, eagerly anticipating the warmth that would greet them inside the pub.

'Grab that table over there,' Jodie gestured to the corner, 'I'll get the drinks.' She turned to Susan, 'except I've no idea what you like.'

'I'll have a Gin and Tonic please.'

'Me too,' Marion added.

The two women squeezed themselves into the corner bench seats and peeled off their coats. Jodie arrived balancing the Gin and Tonics and half a pint of beer between her hands. She managed to set them down on the table without spilling any of them before sliding onto the seat next to Marion. 'Cheers!' She smiled and the three clinked glasses.

'So, I'm sat here with a divorcee and a nearly divorced woman. I hope it's not catching.' She laughed. Kevin was her tall, handsome policeman. How would she cope if he found someone else?

'I don't think you've got anything to worry about as far as Kevin is concerned.' Marion stated. 'You seem to have him under control.'

'Now if this is the part where you blame yourself for Richard's wondering hands, forget it. You're worth ten of him. I didn't believe it when Kevin told me… '

Marion shot her an accusing look. 'What did Kevin tell you?'

Jodie began fiddling with the straps on her handbag; her and her big mouth…

Susan stood up and excused herself to go to the toilet.

Marion moved into her seat so she could look Jodie in the eye.

Jodie knew she could either lie to her friend or be honest with her. Leaning forward, she rested her arms on the table, and looked directly at Marion. 'Kevin saw Richard and a blonde woman together, kissing. Before you get mad at me, you'd already made up your mind to go away. I could see how much you needed a break. I didn't want to spoil it for you at the time so I confronted Richard whilst you were in France. I told him if he didn't come clean I would spill the beans. Thank God, he manned up and told you, so I didn't have to. Although to be fair to him…'

'Fair to him!'

'Hear me out,' insisted Jodie. 'He was upset; he actually broke down in front of me. He told me he regretted it and the affair was over. I don't think he knew about the baby.'

Marion sat back in her seat not knowing how to respond to what she had just heard. Her best friend knew her husband was having an affair and did not tell her.

'Would it have made any difference if you had known before you went to France?' asked Jodie.

'Yes it damn well would!' For the hundredth time since Richard had told her about Clare, she thought about François and what could have been.

'How different my life might be right now. I could be living in France. Do you realise how it feels to have missed an opportunity. It's too late now. Why didn't you say something?'

Marion's eyes glistened with tears. How happy she had been with François. She had buried all those feelings to save her marriage which Jodie knew was already over.'

'I'm sorry,' Jodie said softly. 'If you had told me you'd met someone, I wouldn't have hesitated to tell you what I knew about Richard. I only want you to be happy. Can't you contact this French man of yours? Maybe he'll still want you.'

'Thanks! Marion said. You make it sound so simple, as if I can choose who I want to be with when it suits me. François will have forgotten me, moved on. I made my choice, the wrong one, as it turned out.'

'Why don't you try? The very least it will make me feel better.'

*

Three weeks before Christmas, Marion signed the *decree absolute.* Jake came home from university for the holidays, and Carol insisted that Marion spend Christmas day with them.

'Before you try to wriggle out of it, Mark suggested I invite you. It would seem he has had a touch of the Christmas spirit.'

Festive jumpers were all the rage. Marion bought a red one for Alice with a reindeer on the front and wrapped a box of Milk Tray inside it. The jumper fitted her much better than the last one Marion had seen her in. The weight Alice lost had crept back on, and her long, bright red glittering nails did not go unnoticed either.

For Jake's Christmas present, Marion settled on something more grown up. Each time he came near her the whiff of Jean Paul Gautier brought back happy memories.

After dinner they played *Pictionary,* with Alice and Jake groaning each time it was their aunt's turn. Marion couldn't draw to save her life.

In the early evening, Marion left them to watch the Christmas TV and returned home. Mimi was curled up on the kitchen chair, waiting patiently. Marion picked her up.

The cat pushed her head under her chin and Marion tickled her ears. Last year, Richard and she had cancelled Christmas; they had lost Anna four weeks before. This Christmas, she had no husband. Everything she feared for her and Richard had come true, although she never envisaged it would be at the hands of another woman. Her heart felt heavy, laden with regret.

'It's just you and me now,' she said to Mimi. 'Merry Christmas little girl.'

32

On the eleventh of January, Marion received an unexpected message from Richard. Clare had given birth to a boy, Callum. She was surprised how relieved she felt. Not only had there been no problems, but more importantly to her, the baby was not a girl. It was as if the final link to Richard had been broken. Now she was truly ready to move on.

In March, as the garden came alive with spring colours, Marion decided it was the right time to sell the house. The property was in one of the more affluent parts of Huddersfield; much sort after for its schools and one of the best golf courses the area had on offer. She was confident of a quick and profitable sale.

It left her with only one problem. She had no idea where she was going to live. When she told Richard's father about the sale, he wanted her to move to New Zealand. She would easily get a nursing position, and she had to admit starting again somewhere else was definitely appealing. However, she must not let the temptation of getting away from all her memories cause her to make any rash decisions. It had worked for Richard's father; it did not mean that it would work for her. The best thing she could do would be to take a sabbatical. After, she would decide if living in a foreign country was for her.

*

The rented black Ford Focus crawled slowly up the hill until its occupant was certain he had found the right address. He turned the car into the drive and switched off the engine, surveying the stone cottage in front of him. Stepping out of the car, he ran his hands over his belt ensuring his pale blue shirt was tucked neatly into his jeans. He reached inside for his black jacket and pulled it on; the English spring weather was not as warm as that in France. He strolled down the rest of the drive, took a deep breath and knocked loudly on the dark brown wooden door. Whist he waited he looked down past the side of the house. It had a good view, if you liked to look upon the roof tops of towns. So many building; it felt claustrophobic. He preferred the view he had back home of the sea.

    Marion was on her hands and knees under the stairs when she heard the knock. She cursed, brushed a cobweb from the side of her face and slowly backed out from the confined space. She could only imagine what a mess she looked; so be it. She wasn't expecting anyone important.

    François raised his hand to knock a second time. He heard the door handle turn and lowered his arm.

    The door opened.

    Marion stood in front of him wearing a pair of grey baggy tracksuit bottoms; her white t-shirt had a brown smudge mark, as if she'd been carrying something dirty against her stomach. Her hair looked like a bird had made its nest on top of her head and her face was streaked with what looked like a cobweb.

    She blushed.

    François burst out laughing.

Marion threw her hands up to her face and stared into his deep brown eyes and melted. He seemed more handsome than she remembered.

François stopped laughing and smirked. '*Bonjour* Marion.'

'How did you find me?'

'Véronique. She told me everything.'

Marion recollected the e-mail she had written, pouring her heart out to Véronique, late one evening after she had consumed a few glasses of wine.

Marion composed herself and stepped back so he could enter.

He looked her up and down.

She blushed again and tucked several escaped tendrils of hair behind her ear, knowing it did not make her look any better.

'I can offer you a coffee,' she said, trying to keep her voice steady and to break his gaze.

She filled the machine with water and made two espresso coffees.

'Come in.' She gestured to the living room. 'You'll have to excuse the mess.'

'I can see I've interrupted you. Véronique said you were moving house.'

He followed her and went to stand over by the window, in the very same spot Richard had stood when he delivered his confession.

Marion shivered with apprehension and timidly perched on the end of the sofa, tense and completely at odds with the situation.

'Do you know where you will go next?' he asked.

'No not really. My father-in-law wants me to go to New Zealand. He lives there.'

She knew without looking he was staring at her.

'So you were going to break your promise to me?'

She was forced to give him a questioning look. In a moment of recollection, she remembered their last night together. How if she needed to escape again she promised she would go back to him.

She lowered her eyes. 'It's never that simple is it? Véronique never mentioned you in her e-mails. I presumed you'd found someone else and she was sparing my feelings.'

He left his coffee cup on the window sill and moved to sit next to her. 'Nothing could be further from the truth. There has been and still is no one else.'

He took the coffee cup out of her hands and placed it on the table. 'Will you come back to France with me?' he said, bringing both her hands up to his lips.

When she did not respond, he added, 'I hear there are big spiders in New Zealand.'

She pulled her hands away, laughing.

'I chose Richard over you. I let you go so easily?'

'You did what you had to do. The past is exactly that ... you're past. Leave it there. It's time to get on with the future part of your life. And I'd like to be a part of that, if you will let me? I lost you once ...do you believe in second chances?'

He waited for her to answer, his intense stare made her feel uncomfortable. 'You're hesitating. I'm sorry, it was stupid of me to come here after all this time and expect you to fall into my arms as if nothing had changed.'

She had always considered that starting again just meant moving your life and starting somewhere different. It had never occurred to her that it could also mean a second chance with François. What did she have to lose?

'What about my job? I don't speak French. How will I be able to work?'

I will teach you. We will speak nothing else until you are fluent and we will find out how you can work as a nurse, unless you want to work for me in my bar.'

'Your bar!'

He was smiling. 'My uncle died suddenly and left me some money. Natalie lent me the rest. Probably out of guilt for what she did. Ironically I am now the businessman she always wanted me to be. Someone bilingual as well as beautiful, like you will have no problem attracting the customers.

She smiled coyly. 'I can't just say yes. I have to think about it. They at least speak English in New Zealand.'

'But it's the other side of the world. You would be lost from me forever.'

François was leaning too close; she needed space. She glanced over to the clock on the mantelpiece, aware she had a shift to do later.

'How long are you here for?'

'I go back the day after tomorrow. I'm staying at The Old Golf House Hotel.'

Marion's eyes widened.

'Véronique made the reservation....'

'I have to work the late shift today. The good news is that I'm free all day tomorrow.'

'Then we will talk some more, and you can show me this part of England.'

Marion laughed. 'We won't get far in a day but I have an idea where we can go.'

He stood up; Marion followed him into the kitchen.

'*Á demain*,' he said and kissed her cheek.

After he had left, Marion felt her legs go weak; she sank into the nearest chair. François had been here, in her house, wanting to take her back to France to live. She was shaking and smiling at the same time.

33

Where are we going? François asked.

'Somewhere breathtaking,' Marion replied as she stopped at yet another set of traffic lights.

'Ignore all this,' she swept her hand in front of him.

François observed in silence as they passed supermarkets, shops, offices and more traffic lights than he had seen in a lifetime. Gradually the traffic eased; the road wound through conurbations of stone cottages.

François did not say much until they reached Holmfirth.

'This looks lively and more pleasing to the eye,' he commented unexpectedly.

Marion knew what he meant. Holmfirth was a small, picturesque rural town that sat on the banks of a river. Some of the back streets, between the rows of terraced stone cottages, remained cobbled.

'It's popular with tourists. They made a TV series here, now everyone wants to visit the café and Nora Batty's cottage. It's heaving in summer, as you can imagine.'

Marion drove through the town and out the other side. Gradually, they began to leave any sign of life behind them as they started the steep ascent through open countryside to the top of Holme Moss.

'The Tour de France climbed up here in 2014,' Marion remarked as the road twisted and turned.

'It's not quite the Alps but I can see why they chose it.' Francoise whistled. 'And look at that view.' He craned his neck to look behind him.

'I'll stop in the car park at the top. You can see it better from there. After that, the road descends steeply into the Peak District and the county of Derbyshire.'

There were no other cars on the concrete square at the top of the ascent. Marion parked so they could both stare out of the front window at the rolling green hills that stretched for miles. Below them, tiny clusters of grey stone represented the villages through which she had just driven.

'You're looking at the Pennine Hills, known as the backbone of England because they stretch down the middle and divide west from east. Well, up here in the north they do. Aren't they magnificent?'

Marion never ceased to be impressed every time she came up here. She and Richard used to buy fish and chips from Holmbridge, the last village before the climb, and bring them here to eat.

'We're lucky it's a clear day otherwise all this would be hidden in cloud.'

He took hold of her hand. 'It's impressive but still not as nice as looking out at the Atlantic ocean each day.'

Marion smiled. 'Is that your attempt to woo me back to France?'

'Have you thought anymore about it?'

She had not been able to think about anything else since François turned up on her doorstep yesterday morning.

'I can't just give everything up on a whim. I need to be sure.

'I already know it's what I want, but I am a patient man. I think I have already proved that to you.'

Marion smiled at him. 'Are you hungry?'

'Famished!'

She drove back down the valley and parked in the car park of The Old Bridge Hotel in the centre of Holmfirth. It was a lot more up-market than *Le Marin* where François worked. She hoped he would not be overwhelmed by it.

The dining area had the ambience of a cottage with its beamed ceiling and a beige rush carpet. The menu was extensive, probably too specialised for a foreigner. However, Marion spotted that they served *Moules Mariniére.*

'One for you. Unless you prefer to risk trying something else.'

'I think I'll stay with what I know.'

Marion chose Chicken with Mediterranean Vegetables and basmati rice. François, she remembered, liked to drink wine with his *Moules*; she ordered two glasses of chilled Chardonnay, a large glass for him and a small one for her.

She was eager to ask about Véronique and Pascal.

François chatted happily, telling her the guesthouse was doing well and that they both asked after her often.

'You don't have to talk about it of course, but I should like to know what happened with Richard.'

Marion wished she was not the one driving; she felt the need for another glass of wine. Instead, she poured herself a large glass of water and started at the beginning. She explained how Richard had appeared to have changed from the person he was when she left.

'I really did think I had made the right choice …I know that's not what you want to hear.'

François covered her hand with his. 'Go on.'

Marion took a sip of water. 'It lasted about two months then my world fell apart. He told me he'd had an affair and when I came to France, he realised what I meant to him and ended it …too late. She was pregnant.'

'You know what makes me annoyed about all of this. If you had known about the affair before you came to France, it could all have turned out different for us.'

'Had I known about the affair, I doubt I would have got to France. I came, thinking a break would help mend what was wrong without realising the extent of the problem. After all, here I am now, 'in the know', so to speak, divorced because of it, and considering making a fresh start in New Zealand of all places. We would never have met, had Richard told me earlier.'

'Then perhaps I am the only one to be thankful he kept quiet as long as he did.'

Their food arrived and with it, all talk of Richard stopped. When they had finished, François had to ask, 'Do you see still see him?'

'No. They live twenty miles away, in Leeds. They have a son, Callum. He was born in January.'

Francois caught the brief sadness in her eyes.

'Let's go for a walk,' he announced suddenly, ' after all I am a tourist. You can show me the attractions.'

They meandered around the town in the spring sunshine. Marion explained as best she could what the TV series *Last of the Summer Wine* had been about, finding it hard to describe the comedy behind the Yorkshire characters to a French man.

'When will you decide … if you'll come to France? Can't you give me a clue as what the answer will be?'

'I'll give it some serious consideration. That's the best I can promise for now.'

François beamed.

34

Inside, the car was warm, almost cosy. Outside, the November air, chilled by a north wind; bit hard upon the skin. Richard parked on the opposite side of the road, a few yards from the house he now shared with Clare. He kept the engine running. From there, he could see that downstairs was illuminated whilst total darkness reigned upstairs. This was the norm. Clare would be pacing the floor trying to soothe Callum, waiting for him to return from work, so he could put an overtired baby to bed whilst she poured herself a Gin and Tonic and watched whatever soap opera was on the TV.

Callum was not an easy child to get to sleep. They had tried everything, but he simply did not like being left. Richard often felt himself nodding off at the side of the cot, his hand holding that of a wide-awake baby.

He glanced at the carrier bag on the passenger seat; Clare's orders to go shopping before he came home meant there was nothing for his tea. When Marion was working the late shift, he would often go to the pub rather than cook for himself, he wondered if he could get away with doing that tonight, realising for the second time that day how much he missed Marion. He wanted to see her, only to talk. In his desperation, he had telephoned her earlier at work so she could not put the phone down on him. She could however, have told him to get lost, and that would have been reasonable under the circumstances, instead he was pleasantly surprised, she seemed in a good mood when she told him he could come round tonight.

There were still no lights on upstairs in the house. He put the car in reverse gear and headed for the motorway.

*

'Why didn't you bring him to meet me? We don't get handsome French men coming here very often and you kept him all to yourself. How selfish is that?'

'Very selfish.' Marion laughed at Jodie. 'I'm not letting him anywhere near you. The tales you would tell him about me …'

'So, are you going to live in France? Richard doesn't want you anymore …sorry, that sounded harsh.'

'It's the truth. He's too busy playing happy families.'

'Ooh! I'd love to be a fly on the wall when he finds out you're going to start a new life away from here.'

'I haven't said I'm going to yet.'

'You're mad if you don't.'

'Richard phoned me this morning.'

'Please don't tell me he's missing you and begs your forgiveness.'

'He asked if I would see him. He didn't say why.'

'And what did you reply?'

'That he could come over to the house tonight.'

'I want you to ring me the minute he's gone. We can't have you doing anything stupid like getting back together. You can't fool me. I know you still feel something for him.'

'Even if that were true, the damage has been done. He left for Callum's sake. He isn't going to walk away from him now.'

Mimi chose the exact moment that Richard knocked on the door to climb onto Marion's lap. She had eaten her tea; now, it was time for her evening snooze.

'Sorry, little one, we have a visitor.' She tipped Mimi gently off her.

As she went to open the door for him, Marion felt unusually nervous. They were divorced. What was there left to say each other?

He looked old, tired, more than tired; he looked exhausted. He needed a shave, which was not like the Richard she used to know. He would go nowhere without shaving first. It shocked her to see such a transformation in him.

'How have you been?' he asked.

'I'm fine Richard. Why are you here?'

For a moment, she thought he was going to cry.

'Can I come in?'

She hesitated before moving aside. 'You know your way around.'

She followed him into the living room. Mimi had curled up in the corner of the sofa; she made no attempt to move. He did not live here. This was her spot now.

Richard sat down and stroked her on the back. She flicked her tail in annoyance.

'I saw the 'for sale' sign. Where are you thinking of going?'

'I thought about New Zealand. Or maybe France.' She regretted it the moment she mentioned France.

Richard stared at her. 'To lover boy.'

'That's none of your business. Are you going to tell me why you're here or am I to presume you're just being nosey?'

'You're no more virtuous than me you know. Just because you didn't stay with him. I chose not to stay with Clare in the beginning ...'

'But you did in the end.'

He sat back and closed his eyes for a moment then opened them. 'I made a mistake. Leaving you and going to live with Clare.'

'Don't tell me she's thrown you out and you thought you could come crawling back here.'

'I would never presume that. But for the record, I miss you.'

'Do you want to tell me what's going on?'

Richard ran his fingers through his hair and let out an exasperated sigh. 'Everything I suspected would happen has happened.'

'What do you mean by that?'

'Clare has decided she wants to stay at home and be a full-time mum. By full-time, I mean only the hours I am not around. As soon as I come home from work, she hands Callum over to me. Apparently, he's had enough of her and wants his daddy. How she miraculously knows this since he can't yet speak. She's also too tired to cook in the evening. If I want something to eat, I have to get it myself.'

Marion hid the smile she felt was beginning to form. 'I take it fatherhood isn't all you expected it to be.'

'Guess who has to do the early morning feed on top of getting ready for work.'

This time Marion did not contain her smile. 'So you've come here for sympathy.'

'No. I've come here to tell you I can't live like this. I'm exhausted. I'm leaving Clare.'

'But what about Callum?'

'We'll just have to come to some arrangement.'

'So we went through all of this for nothing. Does Clare know she's about to become a single parent? Because let me tell you something, the reason she wanted you in the first place was to avoid having to bring up Callum alone.'

'Did she tell you that?'

'She might have said she loved you as well.'

'I never loved her, you know. Not like you. Do you think if Clare hadn't got pregnant you could have forgiven me?'

Marion shrugged. 'I don't know. What a mess everything has turned out to be.' She sighed. 'If we'd talked about things after losing Anna, you wouldn't have had the affair, I wouldn't have gone to France; there would have been no Callum and no François. Just the two of us, as it used to be. It's too late now. We can never go back.'

'I am sorry,' he murmured.

Marion looked at him. He had more than a day's growth of stubble on his chin, and his curly hair had taken on a wild look of its own. He was a shadow of the man she once loved.

'I know you are. For once I actually believe you,' she said. 'But its still too late.'

After he had left, she poured herself a glass of wine. It was not her problem if his world was falling apart.

*

Why did he have to find the only car that stuck to the speed limit when he needed to get home? He did not want to go home but life would be even less worth living than it was now if he did not.

He loved his little boy Callum. He loved Marion; always had and always would.

He hated Clare.

Annoyed, he slammed his hand on the steering wheel. A forty-five minute journey ahead of him and a Sunday driver in front of him, except it was Friday.

Friday night. Pub night.

I bet he's drunk, Richard thought. That's why he's driving so carefully. Doesn't want to attract attention. Ludicrous; the police would spot him a mile away.

Whilst he crawled along behind the drunk, he could hear Clare's voice in his head, whining. 'Why are you late? Where have you been? You don't realise how tiring being a mum is.'

As if watching *Pepper Pig* all day was exhausting.

He supposed he should phone and appease her. He felt relieved when he got her voicemail, and left a message. He told her he had been to see Marion and was stuck in traffic. He did not care if it upset her to know he had been with his ex wife. He even smiled at the thought of what conclusion she could make from him saying he was stuck in traffic. How many times had he used that on Marion when he and Clare were carrying on?

He had considered leaving Clare on several occasions. God knows he wanted to. Then he would have a battle over the custody of Calllum.

Clare would win easily. Mothers always did.

Then what?

Visiting rights until she found someone else to fill his shoes. He would see his son less and less. It was no life for a child to have to fit into two separate worlds, pulled from pillar to post, let down constantly. It would be fairer on Callum if he had never been born. Why did he go along with the pregnancy? Marion might still be his wife now if he had not let the past influence him.

Frustrated, he shouted at the other driver. 'Don't you know the police can do you for dangerous driving? You'll cause a bloody accident.'

He saw the on coming lights of the lorry up ahead. They were a distance away.

'For Gods sake! This is a fifty mile zone not thirty.'

The lights were getting closer. He moved out to overtake the car.

35

Richard's father turned the car into the drive. It did not seem like two minutes had passed since they were leaving for the crematorium. Now, they were back home. What Marion had been dreading was over, but not without incident. When she saw Clare at the funeral, she had been so tempted to tell her about the night Richard had come to the house. She was angry with her for being so naïve, so childish and selfish. Whatever Richard deserved, it was not to die.

'Will you stay for a while?' Marion asked Brian. 'At least have a cup of tea with us.'

'Thanks, but I won't, not today. Can we talk tomorrow?'

'Of course. Come for lunch.' She bent over and kissed him on the cheek before opening the car door and stepping out. Carol was already out of the car waiting for her. She raised a hand and mouthed goodbye through the window to him. The two women watched as he drove away.

Many a revelation had taken place in Marion's kitchen over the past year. The solid pine table, bought from a shop in Halifax that specialised in renovating old furniture, and the sturdy carver chairs with their padded green chequered cushions, had often provided a comfortable place to sit and exchange views over a cup of something.

Today was no exception.

Marion finished making the tea, placed the mugs on the table and sat down opposite Carol. Mimi had curled up on the next chair; she glanced up, purring softly when Marion sat down.

'Do you still think Richard took his own life?' Carol said. 'Don't you think you're getting carried away?'

'You didn't see the state he was in.'

'I'm sorry. I just can't feel any sympathy for him. The only one I feel sorry for is Callum. What did he ever do to deserve losing his father? Women like Clare will find someone else. It won't take her long. Let's hope she doesn't wreck another marriage along the way. Are you going to tell her what he told you, about her?'

Marion shrugged. 'What if she jumps to the same conclusion as I did? Think of the regret she'll have to live with. You're not that harsh a person, are you, to wish that upon her?'

'No. But you should be,' Carol snapped.

'What's the point? It's like you said, the only person that matters now is Callum. Would you want Alice or Jake to know that their father ended his life because he felt he'd made a mistake to be with them?'

'Callum doesn't have to know.'

'So Clare will have to lie to him all his life. What she doesn't suspect she can't lie about.'

Carol sighed. 'You're probably right. I seem to be finding it harder to forgive what she did than you. I saw what losing Anna did to you and it still didn't stop Richard from causing you more grief.'

Marion sipped her tea. She appreciated Carol's concern but Richard had ruined two lives, it was time to put a stop to it.

'I have something to tell you that may just change the way you feel,' she told Carol.

Not knowing where to begin, Marion hesitated.

'Don't keep me in suspense,' Carol demanded.

Marion took a deep breath. 'When I went to France, I met someone. He's called François.'

'What! So, you played Richard at his own game. Good for you.'

'No. I didn't know he was having an affair with Clare when I went to France. I guess I just needed someone, like Richard, I suppose.'

'At least you saw sense and came home. You didn't get yourself pregnant and ride off into the sunset.'

Marion laughed. 'No, but you can imagine how I wished I had when I found out about Clare.'

'Why am I the last to know all this?' Carol asked.

'I suppose it felt like I was being a hypocrite at first.'

'So what happened to François?'

'He came to visit me.'

'I don't believe this. Why didn't you introduce him?'

'Don't you start, Jodie was bad enough.'

'What did he want?'

'He came to ask me to go France and live with him.'

Carol's mouth opened wide. 'You can't seriously think of going to live in a foreign country. You can't speak French. What will you do for work? What about me and Alice and Jake?'

'I should imagine Alice and Jake will think it cool to have an aunt living in France. They'll only be thinking of free holidays. And why can't you come and visit?'

'Are you in love with this man, I mean really in love, or are you just flattered by his attentions at your age?'

'Now that's a question I've asked myself many times. When I met him, I was miserable, it felt like I'd lost everything, and I wasn't worth anything. I couldn't keep a baby or a husband. François changed all that. I felt so happy I thought I loved him. But I had Richard, who couldn't stop saying sorry and I believed him. If I had known about Clare, there's no doubt I would have stayed with François.'

Marion stood up and went to stand by the window. There was a small patch of earth to one side of the drive, where daffodils and crocuses would soon emerge, followed by deep red, perfumed roses, in May. She remembered planting every shrub and bulb. Almost twenty years of her life had been spent living in this house. Even though love and laughter had turned to tears and heartache, she would still miss living here. She always believed that life's tragedies either destroyed or strengthened a person. In the beginning, they destroyed her. Now, after everything, she knew that the choice she wanted to make, of being with François, was not the right one. Only now did she have the strength to see that.

She sat back down and took a sip of her tea.

'I'll always be grateful to François, and I'll never regret what we had.'

'But?' Carol queried.

'I don't think I can change my life for him. Do I really want to start again somewhere else without my friends and my family? This is where my roots are. If I'm going to have to start again, here is the best place, with the people I love.'

Mimi chose that moment to unfurl herself and stretch her body, arching her back she quivered slightly before crossing over to curl up once again on Marion's knee this time. 'See, even the cat agrees with me.' Marion smiled.

'So what happens now?' Carol asked. 'Why did you sell the house?'

Before Marion could answer, Carol continued. 'Ever heard of this saying?' She screwed up her face trying to make sure she had remembered it correctly. 'In life there is a B for birth and a D for death.' She paused. 'And in between there is a C for the choices we make as to how to live that life.' She looked pleased with herself for remembering it all.

Marion laughed. 'Who came up with that nonsense?'

Carol felt deflated. 'I thought it was quite good. Anyway who do you think told me?'

'A philosophical teenager called Alice?'

'Maybe there is some truth in it,' Carol stated. 'Isn't it better to say to yourself, I made a mistake than what if?'

'You think I'm making the wrong choice?'

'Don't get me wrong.' Carol reached over and laid a hand on Marion's arm. 'I don't want you to go and live in France, but neither do I want you to make a decision you'll regret.'

'But that could be said for both scenarios.'

'Well then, why don't you compromise? Don't say no to François, just say not yet. He came all this way to find you; you don't know how lucky you are. He's given you hope for the future, not something to fear; a chance to start again.' Carol's eyes widened as she became excited by the whole idea. 'You could take Alice with you. She'll need a job when she's finished her exams. I'm sure she would love to work in a French bar by the sea.'

Marion laughed, although there was a lot of sense in what Carol had just said. She took a deep breath and looked around her. 'I've experienced joy in this house and a lot of pain. I decided to sell it because it's time to say goodbye to the memories and create new ones.' Stroking Mimi's head, she turned to Carol. 'Wherever that maybe.'

Acknowledgements

It has been a pleasure and an experience to write this book, and a box ticked on my bucket list. However, I could not have succeeded alone.

Firstly, a huge thank you to my friend and mentor, James Vance, for his advice and encouragement.

Thanks also to the members of the Novel Writers group, Denise Bloom and Vanessa Whyte, for help with the story line, and to Linda Dining for casting her teachers eye over my work. For her superb author's lunches and writing workshops, I thank Kate Rose.

Finally, I could not end without mentioning my gratitude to Graham, Bethan and Thomas, for allowing me the space to write.

Printed in Great Britain
by Amazon